Paradise Café

& OTHER STORIES

& OTHER STORIES

MARTHA BROOKS

THISTLEDOWN PRESS

Canadian Cataloguing in Publication Data

Brooks, Martha, 1944-
Paradise Cafe and other stories
ISBN 0-920633-57-9

I Title.
PS8553.R66P3 1988   jC813'.54 C88-098152-0
PZ7.B76Pa 1988

Book design by A.M. Forrie
Cover photo by Sean Francis Martin

Typeset by Pièce de Résistance, Edmonton
Set in 11 point Garth Graphic

Printed and bound in Canada by
Hignell Printing Ltd., Winnipeg

Thistledown Press Ltd.
633 Main Street
Saskatoon, Saskatchewan
S7H 0J8

Acknowledgements
The author would like to thank the Manitoba Arts Council for financial assistance; Maureen Hunter, Alice Drader and Kirsten Brooks for generous readings and advice; and Nancy Marcotte and George Toles for helping to bring it all home.

Quotation from "Unchained Melody" by Hy Zaret and Alex North © 1955 Frank Music Corp. © renewed 1983 Frank Music Corp.
International Copyright Secured. All rights reserved. Used by permission.

Quotation from "Chinese Cafe" by Joni Mitchell © 1982 Crazcy Crow Music. All rights reserved. Used by permission.

This book has been published with the assistance of the Manitoba Arts Council.
Thistledown Press acknowledges the support received for its publishing program from the Saskatchewan Arts Board and the Canada Council's Block Grants program.

Down at the Chinese Cafe
We'd be dreaming on our dimes
We'd be playing—
    "You give your love, so sweetly"
One more time
        —Joni Mitchell
        "Chinese Cafe"

For my husband, Brian

CONTENTS

Wild Strawberries

There was nothing they could do about Celine Norman-deau's T.B., the doctors said. It was miliary—the kind that when Uncle Guy was shown the x-rays, he told us, her lungs looked as if she'd been struck by a blizzard. The disease just spread and spread until there was nothing left but white on her x-rays, so maybe that's why it used to be called the white plague at one time, T.B. Anyway, it sure got Celine. And she was only twenty-one years old.

I was not quite seven but they made me go to the funeral. After all, they told me, she would have been your uncle's wife. Don't you remember, Denis, that time she babysat you?

Celine. She sure was beautiful. The most beautiful girl I had ever seen and it was July and she fed me wild straw-berries dipped first into my mother's blue sugar bowl. Fed them to me by hand! With her long white fingers dipping into and out of the fine, shimmering sugar.

She was buried in her wedding dress and everyone said how tragic it was she never got to be married in it.

Shortly after, Uncle Guy met another girl and married her—just like that! You would think he had entirely forgot-ten Celine and how he cried the day she was buried, cried and cried with his big shoulders hunched over and his grey coat flapping against the coffin in the wind. After the funeral, when everyone was drinking coffee—some of the men slipped in whiskey from hip flasks hidden in the trousers of their heavy wool suits and the women bustled about making clucking sounds as they served lunch—Uncle Guy disappeared and nobody went looking for him.

He stayed in his room for two days, hardly ever coming out. He read and re-read all the letters Celine had sent from the sanatorium where she died. I don't know how long after that he did what I remember next, but there he was, out by the backyard incinerator, in full view of the kitchen where my mother was washing up a stack of supper dishes. "Oh, my God! Emile, come quick!" she called to my father, and I came too.

We watched Uncle Guy, his back to us, the door to the incinerator open, as he tossed pages fluttering like white birds into the round rusted opening. As the paper burned, some of the scorched bits were caught by the wind and carried lightly up and out, where they turned a chalky grey before flying off who knows where.

"He's burning her letters," my mother said with a sob. "I don't know how he can do that."

"Life goes on," said my father, his fingers curled at her shoulderblade in a light caress.

Uncle Guy moved out right away and it was then he met the person who would, instead of Celine, become my aunt. My mother didn't like her. "She's English," she said. "She's not one of us." I didn't like her either, but mainly because she wasn't Celine.

The day he moved, my mother gave Uncle Guy an ancient green sofa that used to belong to her mother before she died and joined Grandpère Lagimodière in Heaven. I was angry that Uncle Guy wanted to move. I was angrier still that he took that sofa with him. "It's because of the letters," my mother told me. "Before Celine left for the sanatorium, that was where they courted when Papa and I pretended to be asleep. Your Uncle Guy must take the sofa, you see. I want him to because Celine must never be forgotten."

"I won't forget her," I said, looking into my mother's tired eyes. She hunkered down in her sky-blue housedress and earnestly held me facing her.

"She was only twenty-one," said my mother, "and we all loved her."

Uncle Guy and his new bride were married in our own church by Father Gagnon. My mother, standing beside my father, said, "She isn't even Catholic."

"Hush," my father leaned over. "Her children will be."

One day a couple of years after Uncle Guy was married, I asked him if he ever thought of her. I was sitting on his green sofa. Marianne, my little dark-haired cousin, rosy in her sleepers, sat plumped on his knee and, reaching across the red oilskin tablecloth, dug her pudgy fingers deep into the sugar bowl.

"Ever think of who, Denis?" asked Uncle Guy. He shifted Marianne to his other knee. She snuggled back and sucked her sugary fingers.

"You know, *her*," I said shyly. I was just beginning to notice girls—especially Jeannine M., who sat in front of me at school.

"Who is her?" Uncle Guy smiled at Marianne; she offered one sticky finger for him to kiss.

"Celine," I replied, hardly above a whisper.

A shadow could have passed across my uncle's face and let him out the other side, so like a clown behind a hand he was—one side mirth, the other side tragedy. Marianne struggled off his knee to the floor. She crawled away and he watched as if she had gone farther than he could ever reach. His wife had taken the truck and was at some church meeting.

"Celine died a very long time ago," he told me, just as if I had never been informed of the fact.

"She died two and a half years ago," I said carefully, watching his face.

He picked up his cup and went to the stove for a refill from the grey metal pot. Slowly he turned the burner from low to off. He leaned against the stove and sipped the unsweetened black coffee.

"Mama says we should remember the dead, otherwise it's as if they never lived," I pressed.

"Your mama," said Uncle Guy, "never lets anything alone." His eyes searched for something in the bottom of the cup and found nothing. He came over to the sofa and placed his big hand on my shoulder. "Let go of her, Denis. You can't remember forever, it isn't healthy."

Four more years passed and Uncle Guy and his wife had two more children and Jeannine M. and Marcel Berard got caught skinny-dipping in the creek down the hill from the cemetery. My mother laughed and laughed when she heard that. "Marcel Berard is turning out just like his brother," she said to my father. "Do you remember that Marius? He used to double-date with Guy and Celine. And he got two girls in trouble the year Celine went to the sanatorium."

Saturday afternoons Uncle Guy and his wife went to town. Now I was old enough, occasionally they asked me to babysit. They could then stay a little longer, have supper at the Chinese café, and maybe see whatever movie was playing at the theatre.

In July they asked me, on a day so hot even the birds were too tired to sing. The aunt, her red hair tied up with a yellow chiffon scarf, said, "Make sure you give the baby his bottle at six o'clock sharp, Denis, or he'll fuss and fuss and you'll never get him to settle down." Their truck swayed quickly out of the yard, leaving behind a gritty grey cloud.

It wasn't until just before they were to return home that I found the letter. The babies were in their beds and Marianne had fallen asleep beside me on the sofa. Her head was on my lap; I didn't dare move for fear of waking her. I was so bored. No books were within reach and the radio also was too far away. Absently I shoved my hand down the back of the sofa. I found a bobby pin and then a purple jelly bean. It wasn't too old so I ate it. Closer to me I felt again, hoping for another. Instead, my hand went unexpectedly farther down than even the aunt's ferocious-sounding vacuum cleaner could possibly reach. I felt dust and ancient crumbs, then a slender, ragged envelope. I eased Marianne's damp curly head off my knee and tugged until the soft, yellow envelope surfaced. In feminine flowing hand and pale green ink, it was addressed to Uncle Guy from the sender, C. Normandeau. Celine!

The letter, dated just after she had arrived at the sanatorium, began, "My darling Guy". It told of her fear and her bravery through the everyday life of her days in hospital: the matron did this and that, the doctors were especially kind.

She had made friends with a woman in the next bed, "Think of it, Guy, she has four children. When they visit, they wave to her from the front lawn. Her husband looks so very worried.

"I miss you so very much. Do you remember last summer? That silly duck you chased out of Madeleine Berard's chicken coop? That time Marius tied your shoelaces together while you were kissing me? I hope to be stronger soon. Mom is sending my dress. There is lace left to sew on."

I skimmed the other pages until I came close to the end of the letter. There I stopped as her words began to blur and I could feel my body being consumed by a terrible sickening heat. "Tell Denis, that dear little boy," she wrote, "I had strawberries for lunch today. They were delicious, but not nearly so delicious as those wild ones we picked—does he remember this? And we ate them with sugar stolen from his mother's sugar bowl!"

When Uncle Guy arrived home I was caught between wanting to hit something and needing to find a place to hide. I covered it by telling him that I thought I'd caught the flu. The aunt rushed Marianne off to bed and Uncle Guy drove me home in the Ford truck.

We pulled up to the house and I said to him, "Memories are ghosts, just like people. Even now you are a memory to me."

"What a strange thing to say, Denis," said Uncle Guy. "You will grow up to be a writer or a famous politician, for sure." He smiled and turned off the engine. "Was there something else you wanted to tell me?"

"No." I vehemently shook my head. Even then I almost gave him the letter. It was so quiet in the cab of his truck as he waited for an answer to his impossible question. Eventually I simply left, the metal door closing with a solid sound behind me. I watched until the headlights flickered past trees and out onto the highway. I entered the sleeping house and avoided the creaks in the stairs by sliding up with my back to the wall. In my bedroom, at the bottom of my chest of drawers, I kept a Margeurita cigar box. Such treasures it contained! A spotted loon feather, a giant clay marble, a horseshoe nail ring, a tarnished heart-shaped locket I'd found along the road one day and had never had the courage to give to Jeannine M. I added to these Celine's ragged mooncoloured letter. Then I went to bed and slept very well the whole night long.

Running with Marty

I'm standing on the lawn of this tacky cottage at Wasagaming, watering the grass for Valdeen, Dad's latest girlfriend, when who should walk up the driveway all red and perspiring with a backpack sliding off his shoulder but Martin Faykes.

"Hi Elizabeth," he says, just like he's walked over from a couple of blocks away to see me. He then falls into the chartreuse lawn cart and gasps, "Get me a drink."

"My gawd," says Valdeen when I go into the kitchen, "what a surprise. Why didn't you tell me you'd invited him?"

"I didn't," I reply, and I leave with Marty's Coke.

Marty is the only boyfriend I've ever had. I started going out with him because he asked me. I figured, by grade nine, I was abnormal; nobody I liked had asked me out yet. Marty and I have been seeing each other for almost a year. In that time my dad has split with my Mom and Valdeen is his fifth girlfriend.

This cottage, beside the others that all look alike, belongs to her. She's a widow with a son who's two years older than me and has a summer job, back in the city, at 7-Eleven. Dwayne is too cool to notice me. Probably he's gone through this before, putting up with the children of his mother's latest.

Until my dad started dating he was actually pretty decent. Then he went off his rocker and started dating everything in sight. Valdeen has lasted the longest: four months. I swear he has absolutely no taste. What man in his right mind would get serious over a woman named Val-deen?

We're here at Valdeen's cottage because Dad says I need a normal family vacation. He's talking now as if Valdeen of the Clairol hair is part of our family! I wonder what my Mom would think of that. If she thinks at all, living with that bald fat musician she prefers to her own home.

Marty's parents have sex several times a week and hold hands in Safeway. The longest fight they ever had lasted a day and a half and gave him a nightmare. I told him my parents never fought. In fact, for a year before Mom left, they were hardly ever at home so how could they fight?

Sometimes Marty just makes me want to smack him, the way he worries about everything when it's *my* life that's falling apart.

Marty looks like your typical ninety-eight pound weakling. But he runs fast and has muscles that don't show. His eyes are a peaceful green. He has large lips and not too many zits. Theatre is the biggest thing we have in common. His parents don't go; neither does my dad, and Valdeen—give me a break—thinks Shakespeare is the name of a restaurant. Marty is a track star, likes tinkering with his dad's old truck, and wants to be an actor someday. The first time I saw him, he was wandering around in this finky-looking cape. Some of the kids I know think he's weird, but you just have to get used to him.

I don't mind kissing Marty. He has very convincing lips.

Mom says I should hang onto him, but then she makes bizarre statements like: Friendship is more important than love. And: Never trust a silent man. You really can't count on the opinion of a person who'll break up a sixteen-year marriage without giving some advance warning.

Mom likes Marty. Dad, if he has an opinion, keeps it to himself and mostly ignores him.

"So, what do you think of my earring?" says Marty, as I hand him the Coke.

"Good grief," I say, noticing it for the first time. It's silver with a dangling cross. "What did you go and do that for? It looks pretty dumb."

Marty tugs at the earring. He looks momentarily wounded. Then he brightens and pulls me down beside him on the lawn cart. He puts his arm around me and makes me cuddle up. We sit like that for a while. He chug-a-lugs. I fold my arms, tight, across my chest. We watch the small, whirring lawn sprinkler. It spritzes idiotically around, covering about three feet of lawn. This is why it has to be moved about twenty times to get the whole thing done. It occurs to me that everything Valdeen owns is tacky.

"Terrific lawn sprinkler," says Marty, who thinks of himself as a Renaissance man. "That sprinkler comes right out of the Fifties. Where does Valdeen find such neat stuff?"

I get up and walk over to the tap at the side of the cottage. Icy water dribbles off my hands and down my legs as I shut the thing off.

"Why don't we go for a walk?" Marty suggests, because he sees that I'm a little tense. So we leave, cut across a couple of streets, and go down to the lake. We walk along the beach together. Marty's in no hurry; he's slow as a slug. He breathes expansively, taking in the piney air. I get a little ahead and kick the sand. We don't talk.

At a quiet part along the lake, far from the crowded downtown public beach, we find a sunbleached log and sit. A sailboat with rainbow-coloured sails glides by. I watch Marty watch the sailors—a man and a woman in identical white shorts and tops and wearing orange life preservers. Marty waves. They wave back.

I say to him, "Marty, I think we should break up." Simple as that. And the smile he's been wearing slides from his face like water off a rock.

"I've been thinking about it for quite a while," I say,

looking at the sailboat as it edges away. "I think, you know, we're too young to get serious."

"What do you mean?" he says, his voice sort of dead. "I thought we were serious."

"It's better," I say, ignoring this, "if we see other people." I turn my head back and continue, "Even my mother thinks so."

This of course is a lie but I need all the ammunition I can get.

"Your mother ran out on you," says Marty, "when you were in bed with chicken pox. Hey! Look at me." He's smiling like crazy now, but tears have started to tremble along the lower rims of his eyes. "Don't you think I know what you're scared of? Elizabeth, I came all this way—for you. Holy cripes, what more do you want?"

I suggest coldly, "Maybe we could be friends?" Marty all of a sudden gets to his feet, grabs a stone off the beach, and chucks it hard into the lake.

I follow him back to the cottage. Valdeen comes out wiping her hands on the hem of an apron that says, "Over Forty and Feeling Foxy." She looks at him, then at me, then back at him, and says, "You staying for dinner, Marty?"

"Valdeen," I say with a withering sigh, "he's hardly going to go back to the city *now*—it's a hundred and sixty miles away."

Marty, looking tired and white, says angrily, "Yeah. I'm going." He snatches his backpack off the lawn cart.

"But the bus doesn't leave until seven o'clock," I protest.

He's hauling the pack over his skinny, wirey frame as he says, "I didn't take the bus. I hitchhiked."

Next thing I know, I'm catching his shadow as he quickly vacates Valdeen's property.

Hands in her apron pockets, Valdeen eyeballs me and says in the coldest voice I've ever heard come out of her, "Elizabeth, you are one dumb kid. If you let that nice boy hitchhike back to the city, you are going to hate yourself for a very long time."

"I already do," I say, crying. I start for the cottage. But

she takes hold of me with those hands of hers—the ones with the long purple nails—and wheels me around to face her. "It's time you started thinking of somebody else's misery instead of enjoying your own so much," she says. "Your dad allows it. Your mom allows it. But I'm not going to allow it."

"You can't make me do anything," I snap back. "It's my life. You can't run it."

"Oh yes I can. You stay right here. Don't move." Valdeen goes into the cottage for her cigarettes. Coming back, she hollers at my dad, "Elizabeth and me are going out. If we're not back in ten minutes, check on that stuff in the oven."

My dad, probably from the chair where he's always reading, calls, "Wait. Where are you going?"

"None of your beeswax," replies Valdeen. She hauls off her apron, tosses it over the back of the lawn cart. I am ushered, by my elbow, out to the car.

"So what am I supposed to say to him?" I ask. Valdeen starts the engine. Hangs a Craven M out of her purple-to-match-the-nail-polish mouth. "You're a smart kid for somebody so dumb," she says. "Just start talking. It'll come to you."

We back speedily off the driveway. Away down Ta-Wa-Pit Drive is Marty Faykes, running very fast and looking very small.

Behind a cloud of mentholated smoke, Valdeen mutters, "Damn," shifts, and steps on it.

When we're almost on him, Marty stops running, turns, sticks out his thumb, sees it's us, turns around, and runs again.

I'm hanging out the open window as something small and fierce breaks inside me. "Marty! Stop!" I yell.

"Why?" he says. We're right beside him now. "Give me one good reason."

"Please stop. I have to talk to you."

"You've already done that," he says, and looks straight ahead. He's breathing hard. His runners make a smacking sound on the pavement. Balls of perspiration have begun to course down his face.

"I didn't mean it," I tell him. "You're right. I'm really scared and it makes me crazy, but I'm okay now. Okay, Marty?"

Out near the curb, pushing a weed bar, is a lady with stiff beauty parlour hair. She gives us a look, frowns as we pass— Marty puffing, me begging. Valdeen smiles sweetly and gives her a slow, queenly wave from the elbow.

"Please Marty," I say, "I don't want you to go." My mother has always been of the opinion that I take her good advice for granted.

He slows up a bit. Valdeen furiously flicks ashes out of her window. "You getting out?"

"Yes," I say. "Stop this car."

"Suits me fine," she says, and pretty soon I'm outside running with Marty.

Later, Dad sits at the table and glowers over his dinner. Valdeen has another cigarette going beside the stove. She serves Marty next. With shrill gaiety she tells him, "This'll put meat on your bones!" and she eases a double helping of Pigs-in-a-Blanket onto his plate.

Marty gives her a smile like he's deeply grateful. He forks a sausage out from under its blanket of dough, suspiciously rolls it over on his plate, inspects it briefly like it's a small turd.

Valdeen says uncertainly, "It's my specialty."

I sigh and say, "Marty, I'd like some ketchup."

He reaches over with the plastic squeeze bottle, then right in front of Valdeen and my scowling father, squirts a slow artistic heart onto the middle of my plate.

The Way Things Are

Ernie is every bit as smart as that barn cat we let into the house last fall," Fudgo remarked as he helped me hang out the wash for our mother, who was pregnant again.

Fudgo—that's what we called him because he had a fudge-coloured birthmark on his right cheek—handed me the other end of a tablecloth the same pale green as cattails when they first sprouted out of our slough in the spring.

The flapping cloth attacked me as I struggled to attach it, with wooden pegs, to the line. I stood back to watch it billow up like a parasol.

"Cats aren't smart," I said, to show Fudgo I knew just how smart Ernie wasn't.

"They absolutely are," said Fudgo, because he was a year and three months older than me and liked to think he was right about everything. "Especially barn cats and strays. That fat cat of ours wouldn't ever leave the house except that he gets tossed out on his ear a couple of times a day. You'll notice how he's back in ten minutes flat." He reached into the wicker laundry basket, withdrew a wet pillowcase, and shook out the crinkles. "He knows," Fudgo continued, with a critical eye on a seam I'd mended badly, "there's nothing comes close to three squares a day and a warm place to sleep."

"Are you saying Ernie is never going to leave us?" I whipped the pillowcase out of his hand.

"Not unless the house burns down," said Fudgo, with a self-satisfied smile. "I'd be willing to bet on it."

I didn't like Ernie or the cat. Although I had to admit I liked the cat a little better; it didn't have a runny nose or swollen sad eyes, and it didn't have to be told to take a bath. Taking a bath was all it ever did! Lick, lick, lick all day long on the afghan in the brown rattan chair.

Ernie had worked at a few other farms before coming to us and each time, for reasons that were never quite made clear, had soon returned to the school.

It was rumoured that his mother was Isobel Yates, the anemic, unmarried daughter of Percy Yates, who was a retired widower and former owner of one of the three gas stations in town. Isobel was a bit odd herself, so it was pretty easy to see how Ernie might be her son.

He didn't act like anybody's son, though; he just shadowed the heels of anybody who encouraged him with a glance or a word.

If what Fudgo said was true, if he wouldn't ever leave us, I guessed he'd be one of the family. This was an intolerable idea. What with me, Fudgo, the twins, and the other on the way, there was hardly a corner of the house to call your own. The previous hired man had stayed until he'd become old and ill, and died.

Ernie was only twenty years old and clearly very healthy. In spite of a weary procession of meals, which with cooking and dishwashing all seemed to run together, he ate each as if it were his last. His pouchy eyes scanned the nearly empty serving dishes—a scabby potato here, three or four green beans there—and the milk puddle at the bottom of the pitcher. He would wipe his hands slowly over his pant-legs, then dolefully lever his fleshless back away from the table.

Once, following dinner about a week after he came to us,

Mother caught him stuffing half a dozen sour milk buns into his gaping jacket pockets.

"Ernie," she said, vaguely chiding, "are you still hungry?"

"No no. Good meal. You bet, you bet," he said, wagging his silly head.

"Then why did you steal those buns?"

"Didn't steal. No no. Save 'em for later." He smiled a smile that just missed being engaging. It seemed the dentist at the school hadn't wasted time or money filling teeth; he simply pulled them.

"We have to be patient with Ernie," she told me later, "and *kind,* Marina."

I sashayed away to the cupboard, where I shoved the plate I'd just dried into a pyramid of plates so that they all groaned and clattered together.

All summer long food disappeared from the kitchen. As it was my job to make the beds every morning, I had to brace myself for whatever I might find under Ernie's pillow.

Mother said, "Poor Ernie. Somewhere in his life he's learned to hoard food against a rainy day."

I suppose it was inevitable that he and the cat would become friends. At first its pale amber eyes followed him everywhere. Next thing we knew that cat, curled up on the afghan, would get slowly up, stretch and heavily plop to the floor as Ernie, with pathetic eagerness, made room for it on his lap.

He began to say goodbye to it on his way out to the barn every morning. At noon, as he entered the mud room off the kitchen, he'd call to Mother, "Jessie! Where's my cat?" He hardly needed her answer because the thing would hear and actually come on the run, its fat belly wagging back and forth across its toes.

Ernie would pick it up and scratch its frost-mangled ears. Then the two of them would sit like a couple of potato bags and wait for the noon meal.

If it hadn't been for Ernie, I suppose the cat would never have voluntarily left the house. The first morning it trotted after him out to the barn, we were so surprised you could have knocked us over. The only one who wasn't surprised was Dad. "Ernie's real good with horses," he said. "He's slow to learn, for sure, but we've all got to have something special to give in this world, otherwise there's no point in being here at all."

The twins took to following Ernie everywhere too. Only they were up to no good. They'd clamber up to the loft and wait until he and the cat were just below. Then they'd hurl over armloads of hay that sent the cat scattering. Ernie would waggle his head, shuffle off, get a pitchfork, clean up. Dad caught them one day and gave them both a licking, but it didn't have much effect. Being redheads, they were live-wires. They just went underground and found other ways to torment Ernie. I might not have liked him, but it gave me no particular pleasure to see him treated that way. Especially since—and I had to give him credit for this—he seemed to take it all so well and didn't complain to anyone. Maybe he was too dumb to figure out it was they who put dead mice in the fence paint and horseshoe nails in the turpentine and once barbered the cat by cutting off its whiskers so it looked like Hitler, but in his limited way he knew somebody had it in for him.

After the barber job, Ernie cradled the cat in his lap all during supper and muttered forlornly, "Cats gotta have whiskers. That's what makes them cats."

Later Fudgo backed the twins up against the tractor, held them by their shirtfronts, and announced into their startled pink faces that if they didn't quit they'd be walking to school come September—he'd personally see to it. They pleaded innocence and the teasing stopped for a while, but one day the cat mysteriously fell into the rain barrel, so I guess they didn't mind the walk after all.

Ernie wasn't so dumb though. After that he attached himself to Fudgo and wherever he was working, Ernie contrived to be helping out there too, with the cat on a nearby fence licking its toes in the sunshine or following along at the edge of the field, where it dropped every so often to roll its fat body around in the earth.

Sometimes life surprises you by giving you exactly what you've foolishly wished for. Like the time when Grandma (who complained endlessly and loved the family passionately) came for a visit and died unexpectedly. Mother found her that way just as she was bringing her a breakfast tray with the soft-boiled egg she'd wished she hadn't had to make because everybody else had already eaten fried eggs.

What happened to Ernie right out of the blue was one of my life's surprises.

I don't know how Mr. Yates came to know Ernie was living with us, or why anybody would bother to tell him. One hot afternoon in late August, he came rolling up our driveway in the old car he'd had for about twenty years and only ever drove on Sundays when he and his strange daughter, Isobel, went for a drive after church.

This day Isobel wasn't with him and he wore his black Sunday suit even though it was the middle of the week. His white, thinning hair was slicked back, his chin grizzled with day-old stubble. With a kind of guarded dignity he paused momentarily, his foot resting on the old Ford's running board, while he surveyed our land with pale, watery eyes.

"If you're looking for Dad," said Fudgo, "he's up at the tool shed, by the barn."

I was helping outside that day. Ernie stood by with sidewise glances at Mr. Yates. He fiddled with a piece of baler twine, wrapped it round and round his warty oil-stained fingers.

"Thank you kindly," said old Yates. If he'd worn a hat he'd surely have tipped it. Then he nodded hello to Ernie.

The sun dipped behind a lamb-shaped cloud and came out again, hot as ever.

"Don't know that old bugger," said Ernie gruffly. He spat a whole mouthful of glistening tobacco juice right on the spot where Mr. Yates had stood before he left it to walk, straight-backed, up to see Dad.

A little while later Yates appeared again, trudged down the dirt knoll from the barn. Then with a stiff, solemn wave he got into that spit-and-polish vehicle of his and drove off.

"What was that all about?" said Fudgo, removing his hat. With a quick backhand swipe he caught the sweat before it rolled into his eyebrows.

The cat appeared from the tall grasses. A stringy tail and two limp mouse legs dangled from his mouth. With deliberate pride he set the dead thing at Ernie's feet.

"I'll be darned," Fudgo cackled. "Next you'll be teaching him to bring home ducks." He slapped Ernie's boney back. It was the first time I ever saw Ernie catch a joke.

The following morning Fudgo came into my room without knocking, sat on the edge of my bed, and watched as I knotted an elastic around my ponytail. "What's up?" I said to his worried reflection in the vanity mirror.

"Ernie's leaving us."

"Who says?" I swung around to face him.

"He's going to live with Yates and Isobel."

"Yates! That old bugger?"

"What're you so sore about?" Fudgo slapped at a cowlick that always stood up at the back of his head. "Right from the very start, you never liked him."

"Fudgo—you fool," I said, dropping my hands to my lap. "What's that got to do with anything? I don't always like you either."

It took a day for anybody to tell him. Even the twins, who'd found out, shut up about it.

"It's like a bloody funeral in this place," said Dad, after Ernie had taken off up to his room and locked himself in with the cat.

"What right have they?" said Mother.

"Jessie, he isn't yet twenty-one."

"But the school has legal custody. That's what you, yourself, said."

"Doesn't matter. The Yateses never gave up guardianship. That's the way things are. Nothing anybody can do."

"After all these years!" Mother retorted. "They didn't care enough to look after him when he needed them. Now they want his free labour, they're taking him back again."

"Yates is old," Dad argued feebly.

Mr. Yates came around to collect Ernie and his few belong-ings. He maneuvered and wheedled him into the back seat of the car where Ernie sat rigid, arms clasped like sticks between his knees, and wouldn't look up when we said goodbye.

After that the cat ate two bowls of food and sulked and wouldn't sleep on the afghan and peed on the sofa at the end where Ernie had always sat.

Ernie, we were told by concerned neighbours, was behav-ing badly as well. It was reported that twice he'd called Isobel cuckoo, or a hen's behind, or some such thing, and had kicked Mr. Yates very hard in the shin when asked to mow the lawn. The final straw came when he set fire to the garage. They packed him up in the vintage vehicle (which, miraculously, had been wrested from the flames) and drove him back to the school. Apparently this was usual behavior for Ernie, who'd always had a foul mouth and been quite a handful for his employers.

When Dad phoned the school to ask if we could have him back, we all scattered and got busy. Fudgo ushered the twins out to the barn to help clean some machinery; mother clicked away with her knitting needles in the living room; and I got down on the floor and managed to grab one paw of the cat, who was hiding, his eyes all mean electric fire, under the sofa.

A Boy And His Dog

My dog is old. And he farts a lot. His eyes are constantly runny on account of he's going blind. Sometimes when we go for his walk he falls down. We'll be moving right along, I'll feel an unexpected tug at his leash and bingo! he's over. The first time it happened he cried, sort of whimpered, and looked at his leg, the back one, the one that had betrayed him. I crouched in the tall grass (we take our walks in a sky-filled prairie field near the townhouses where we live) and felt the leg, which was in a spasm. I told him if it didn't work too well to just give up for a while. He seemed to know what I was telling him because he looked at me, whimpered some more, and finally flopped his head back on my leg. That's what kills me about dogs. They figure you're in charge of everything. Like if you pointed your finger, you could make a house fall down. Or if you told them everything's going to be okay, it would be.

After a couple of minutes he stood up and took off again in that business-like, let's-get-the-show-on-the-road manner of his, sniffing, squatting to pee (he doesn't lift his leg anymore) near every bush in sight. Later, I found out he fell over because of arthritis. "Nothing you can do, really," said the vet, patting Alphonse's broad flat head. "He's just getting old, Buddy.'' She gave me some red pellet-shaped arthritis pills and sent us home.

After that, whenever he fell, he'd look quite cheerful. He'd lick the leg a bit, hang out his tongue, pant, and patiently wait. Just before stumbling to his feet, he'd look up like he was saying thank you—when I hadn't done anything!

I couldn't let him see how bad all this made me feel. He's so smart sometimes you have to put your hands over his ears and spell things so he won't know what you're talking about. Things like cheese, cookie, walk. All his favourites.

Mom said, ''He can't last forever. Everybody dies sooner or later. It's the natural course of events. And big dogs don't live as long as little dogs.''

Around our house, nobody put their hands over my ears.

Alphonse was a present for my first birthday. Dad brought him home, just a scruffy little brown pup someone was giving away. No special breed. I still have a snapshot of him and me at the party. I was this goopy-looking blond kid in blue corduroy overalls and a Donald Duck T-shirt. Alphonse was all over me in the way of puppies. I'd been startled by Dad's flash and also by Alphonse, who'd chosen that exact moment to paw me down and slurp strawberry ice cream off my face and hands. Dad says I didn't cry or anything! Just lay bug-eyed on the shag rug with Alphonse wiggling and slopping all over me. We got on like a house on fire after that.

Which is why it's so unfair that I'm fourteen going on fifteen and he's thirteen going on ninety-four.

I guess I thought we'd just go on forever with Alphonse being my dog. Listening when I tell him stuff. When he goes, who am I going to tell my secrets to? I tell him things I wouldn't even tell Herb Malken, who is my best friend now that we've been in this city a year. My dad's always getting transferred. He's in the army. When I grow up that's one thing I'm not going to be. In the army. I won't make my kids move every three years and leave all their friends behind. Which is one thing I *am* going to do: have more than one kid when I get married.

There's a big myth that only children are selfish and self-centred. I can say from personal experience that only children are more likely to feel guilty and be too eager to please. It's terrible when you are one kid having to be everything to two parents.

Which is why Alphonse is more than just a dog, you see. Mom even sometimes calls him "Baby". Like he's my brother. Which it sometimes feels like.

Last week he had bad gas. I always sleep with the window open. Even so, it got pretty awful in my bedroom.

Alphonse doesn't make much sound when he farts. Just a little "phhhht" like a balloon with a slow leak and there's no living with him. I swear when he gets like that it would be dangerous to light a match.

I sent him out. He went obligingly. He's always been a polite dog. I listened, first to his toenails clicking over the hardwood floors, then to the scratching of his dry bristly fur as he slumped against the other side of the bedroom door. When you can't be in the same room with someone who's shared your dreams for thirteen years, it's hard to get properly relaxed. It isn't the same when they aren't near you, breathing the same air.

For the next few days he lay around more than usual. I thought perhaps he was just overtired (even though I hadn't been able to stand it and had begun to let him back into my room, farts and all). By Sunday, Mom cocked her head at him and said to Dad and me, "I don't like the way Alphonse looks. Better take him back to the vet, Buddy."

Mom works at the army base too. It's late when she and Dad get home and by that time the vet is closed for the day. So I always take Alphonse right after school. It isn't far—three blocks past the field.

Monday was the kind of fall day that makes you breathe more deeply—the field all burning colours, far-off bushes little flames of magenta and orange, dry wavy grass a pale yellow, and the big sky that kind of deep fire blue you see only once a year, in October. Alphonse didn't fall down once. Eyes half closed, he walked slowly, sniffing the air to take in messages.

A young ginger-coloured cat slithered under a wooden fence and into the field. It saw Alphonse and suddenly crouched low, eyes dark, motionless. For a minute there I didn't think he would notice it. Then his ears went up and his head shot forward. Next thing, he was hauling me along at the end of his leash, barking himself into a frenzy. The cat parted the grass like wildfire and, reaching the fence, dug its body gracelessly under at a spot where there seemed hardly an inch between wood and solid earth.

Alphonse has that effect on cats. They must think he's death on wheels the way they scatter to get out of his way. He stared proudly in the direction of the fence; his nose hadn't failed him. He walked on, a little more vigour in his step, his tongue lolling out, his ears nice and perky.

We reached the edge of the field where we usually turn around on our walks. This time, of course, we didn't. He lost some of his bounce and trailed slightly behind. I looked back. He lowered his head. "She's not going to do anything to you, you crazy dog," I told him. "She's going to shake her head again, and tell us to go home." He kept pace with me after that. Like I said, dogs believe everything you tell them.

The vet is the kind of person whose job runs her life. One minute she's smiling over a recovering patient, or one who's come in just for shots; the next, she's blowing her nose like the place is a funeral parlor. It must be murder to become so involved with your patients. She always looks as if she needs some place to hole up for a good sleep. And her legs are magnets for strays who are forever up for adoption.

At the clinic, I sat down with Alphonse resignedly backed up between my knees. To my astonishment, a resident cat sauntered over and actually rubbed against him. Alphonse sniffed its head and then ignored it (he only likes cats who run). He watched the door to the examining room and trembled. I wondered if his eyesight was improving. With one hand I held his leash; the other I bit away at because of hangnails.

When the vet, smiling, summoned us, I got to my feet and

Alphonse reluctantly pattered after me. Inside the examining room he pressed against the door, willing it to open. I picked him up and lugged him over to the table.

"He's lost weight," said the vet, stroking, prodding gently.

"He was too fat," I said, patting his stomach.

She laughed, continuing her way down his body. "Has he been on a diet?"

"No. I guess older dogs don't eat as much—like older people."

She looked at his rectum. "How long has this been here?" she said softly, more to herself than to me.

"This what?" I looked.

"It's quite a small lump," she said, pressing it hard.

Alphonse stood politely on the table, shaking and puffing.

"Sometimes," she said, with a reassuring smile, "older dogs get these lumps and they usually aren't anything to worry about, Buddy."

Usually? What did she mean, *usually?* My heart began to race.

"Older neutered dogs," she continued, in the same even tone, "very often get benign lumps in the anal region. But we'd better check this out, anyway..."

My dog has cancer. What do I tell him now? What am I going to do? Mom and Dad have left it up to me. The vet, with strained sad eyes, says the little lump is just a symptom of what's going on inside. Why didn't I notice that he was so short of breath? That he was peeing more than usual? That he didn't eat much? That his bowels weren't working? She tells me that when dogs are old all of these things become a problem, it's the usual progress of aging. Except not in Alphonse's case. But how would I know that? I shouldn't blame myself. She says there was nothing I could have done to stop it, anyway.

So what do I tell him? Is he in pain? I couldn't stand it if he were in pain. Tonight Mom wanted to give me a sleeping pill. I refused it. Alphonse is here with me on my bed. He's going to sleep with me one last time. I'll hold him and tell him about me and what I plan to do with my life. I'll have to lie a little, fill in a few places, because I'm not *exactly* sure. But he has a right to know what he'll be missing. I'll have a good life, I know it, just like he's had. I'm going to tell him about it now, whisper it in his ear, and I won't leave out a single detail.

King of the Roller Rink

He was one of the handsomest boys I'd ever seen. Somebody said he was part Indian, and with his powerful, dark good looks and eyes blue and brooding as thunderclouds, I thought of him as some kind of bird god in disguise. He had money, or at least his family did. On those cool summer evenings in that resort town on the only mountain (or what prairie people like to call a mountain) within a thousand miles, he wore white sweaters that looked like they cost the earth and he didn't rent those metal skates the skinny key boys would fit, then clamp, to your runners. He wore his own boot skates made of richly glowing leather, and he was king of the roller rink.

We skated around the edges of the outdoor rink with the sunken concrete floor and the floodlights and, above, the black pine-scented sky that seemed somehow less real than the loud speakers that blared "Wake up Little Suzie" and "Teen Angel" as we clung to each other and shrieked with desperate laughter, hoping Karl the King would notice us.

But he skated every number with Sheila-Rae in her shorts and tight-fitting orlon sweaters. Every night she rented expensive white boot skates to compliment his brown ones. He seemed extraordinarily pleased with her prettiness, her blondeness, as he spun her easily around the floor with a cool hawk-like arrogance that took my breath away.

I was fourteen, underdeveloped, and wore my hair over my eyes as much to hide as to look mysterious. Sheila-Rae was everything I wasn't; her hair and makeup and body seemed flawless. But if I squinted my eyes to block out the other skaters, I could almost imagine it was me holding hands with Karl the King around and around the small crowded floor as everyone scattered to keep from being mowed down by our beautiful, quick, steadily pumping feet.

After each number, Karl and Sheila-Rae floated back to the front of the rink. Kids who weren't skating milled around there on the rough wood platform, or rolled and stumbled back to the booth near the ticket stand, where they bought drinks and cellophane bags of Cheezies.

Karl and Sheila-Rae never seemed to eat or drink. They just skated as if that's all they were made for. When the music started up again, with two or three kicks they were off, and you got the feeling from the way she looked up and smiled into his face that she would have given her soul to make that summer last forever.

Lizzie Keyes and I had purchased identical five-year diaries at the Log Cabin Gift Shop, where fat American ladies hunted down teacups, hand-painted with Mounties or maple leaves. And each night under hissing street lamps we sighed, rolling our eyes, before we separated to be alone with Karl on the crisply lined pink paper. Next day, as we lazed back in her sweaty pine-log room with a picture of King George over the bed, Lizzie would read, "Last night, when Karl skated by? I swear, he looked over and smiled right at me. It was right between "Deep Purple" and "Party Doll." Please, God, make this be a sign!"

In the white heat of day, along the beaches or in the little stores open only during tourist season, we never spied Karl or Sheila-Rae. It was as if, moth-like, they hid their gorgeous flight, appearing only when the music and the floodlights and the dark, cool, rusty-red painted floor of the roller rink lured them out to skate again.

The first time I saw Sheila-Rae up close, she wore shorts and a powder blue sweater. A white stretchy hairband drew her medium-length hair off her forehead and she glowed and chatted animatedly with three fascinated boys who kept a slight distance from her. Karl had just taken off for an unaccustomed round by himself. He skated backwards, hands in his pockets. His hair was so short and perfectly groomed, it barely moved in the little breeze he made. It was then I noticed Sheila-Rae had a small ketchup stain on the front of her sweater, a sweater that closely resembled one I had seen for sale at Woolworth's. She shivered. The sweater was thin. She hadn't skated enough yet to work up much heat.

Over one of the many white sweaters he owned, Karl wore a silky jacket that bore the letters of a university I didn't recognize. Lizzie, who wasn't especially bright, kept saying that those weren't his initials. A short, sweaty boy who had been tagging after her all night informed us that Karl's parents sent him to a university in the States. Karl, he said, was nineteen years old!

At that moment he seemed as unattainable to me as the boot skates I longed to own but knew my parents would never consent to buy for me.

Sheila-Rae stood talking to the boys, who playfully shoved one another and grinned like maniacs into her open smiling mouth. Karl, cruising the rink with hooded eyes, suddenly swooped into the crowded sidelines and appeared seconds later with a girl who wasn't much older than me. Her teeth were unbearably white against her summer tan. Her straight, slim legs flashed above rented boot skates. She flirted with Karl as if she'd been doing it all her life. They sailed past Sheila-Rae. Karl waved. The girl smiled her triumph, then gave a little squeal and clutched at him, having temporarily lost her balance.

Sheila-Rae said goodbye to the boys. They gawked after her as she slowly rolled back onto the rink and skated out the rest of "Heartbreak Hotel" on her own.

Karl skated three more songs with the legs-and-teeth girl, and Sheila-Rae swirled and dove through the crowds, passing them several times, each time with increasing vigour and power and what looked to be sheer joy.

On the fourth song Karl dumped his new partner, who went off the rink and sulked on a bench. She made a show of removing one boot as if it were causing her great pain. She snapped at one of the key boys to bring her another and he, pimply, Brylcreem-slicked, in a gaping unbuttoned shirt, snarled back to get it herself.

Karl whisked around the rink after Sheila-Rae. She executed a graceful arabesque just before he caught up, then she quickly spun around, laughing, to face him. She skated backwards, her hips swaying slightly with the movement. Karl reached out and placed his hands on her waist. They skated together right off the floor. Minutes later they disappeared into the night.

For the next two nights they didn't show. We'd leave early and saunter down the street to the fish 'n' chip shop, then to the café crowd at the Totem Pole—a log-style barn of a building that sold the best fries in town and played the hottest music. But Karl and Sheila-Rae weren't in either place. They'd vanished like a dream, leaving us vaguely frustrated and unsatisfied.

On the third evening, Karl showed up late at the roller rink in the company of a boy whose silk jacket bore the identical letters to his. The two sleek girls with them wore shorts and heavy Nordic ski sweaters. Close up, their skin, with makeup softly defined, was the colour of scrubbed peaches. One collided with, then pushed past me. Her soft sweater grazed my sweaty, bare arm. I turned to say "Sorry," or something stupid like that, but she was laughing attractively at nothing in particular, so I didn't bother. I noticed her citrus-smelling perfume; she was the type who would dab it on her sweater. The whole effect of her made me miserable with longing for a skiing holiday in Banff, a place I'd only ever heard about.

Karl had rented boot skates for his friends. I struggled with a heavy clamp-on skate that had suddenly left my runner during "Stupid Cupid." Then I whizzed back to the floor so I could be there to watch them come on.

Just as I thought, these girls didn't know how to skate. Instead, they flapped and fluttered around like land-marooned swans, gold bangle bracelets shimmering on their slender wrists beneath the false lights of the rink. They laughed, clinging to Karl and his friend. The friend skated well but with no heart-stopping style.

Sheila-Rae appeared half an hour later, her hair done up in a tight blonde bun. I skated away from Lizzie, mumbling some excuse, and went to the newly arrived skaters at the benches. I plunked down near a key boy who was in the middle of trying to explain to a drunk why the clamp-ons he'd rented wouldn't fit on the shoes he was wearing. Loose-lipped, the drunk listened for a while, then insisted that he *always* skated in cowboy boots. Across from us, Sheila-Rae came and seated herself and frowned over the laces of her rented boot skates. Her makeup base was too dark, too orangey; a little bit had rubbed off onto her white turtleneck sweater. The drunk cowboy leered at her legs and asked where she'd got those nice boots. I wanted to tell her to go into the washroom and scrub and scrub until she glowed like the night I'd seen her up close in the pale blue sweater with the ketchup stain. I wanted to warn her about those untouchable girls who were not like us, but then Sheila-Rae got to her feet, swept grandly past, and headed out to the manic activity on the roller rink floor.

The girl with the citrus-smelling perfume skated with Karl. They looked like models who'd just stepped from between the pages of a magazine. She had released his arm and he now had a friendly grip on her hand. All of the passion and arrogance had gone from his skating. It briefly occurred to me that maybe she was his sister or a cousin, but Sheila-Rae rolled slowly past and the girl looked after her, then quickly up into the mask Karl had made of his face. She made him let go of her hand so she could cling to his arm again.

But the strangest sight of all was Sheila-Rae as she skated around and around that rink not looking up, not noticing

Karl. Between songs, when everyone else stopped skating, she kept right on like she didn't have a care in the world. And from far away, under those lights, when you didn't know her makeup was wrong and had made a stain on her thin white sweater, she looked and skated like a queen.

What I Want to Be When I Grow Up

On the third Thursday afternoon of every month, I take my mother's hastily written note to the office where the school secretary, Mrs. Audrey Plumas, a nervous lady with red blotchy skin, looks at it and tells me I can go. Then I leave George J. Sherwood Junior High, walk down to the corner, and wait for the 2:47 bus which will get me downtown just in time for my four o'clock orthodontic appointment.

I hate taking the bus. It's always too hot even in thirty-below-zero weather. The fumes and the lurching make me sick. The people are weird.

Mom says with the amount of money she's forking out to give me a perfect smile I shouldn't complain. "Andrew," she says cheerfully, "taking the bus is an education. It's a rare opportunity for people of all types and from all walks of life to be in an enforced environment that allows them to really get a close look at one another." She then adds, meaningfully, "Think of it as research for your life's work." She goes on like that even though she can't possibly know what she's talking about because she's a business executive who drives a brand new air-conditioned Volvo to work every day.

I made the mistake, a while ago, of telling her I want to be a journalist when I grow up. Out of all the things I've ever wanted to be—an undersea photographer, a vet for the London Zoo, a missionary in Guatemala—she feels this latest choice is the most practical and has latched onto it like it's the last boat leaving the harbour.

She feels that, at fourteen, I have to start making "important career choices." This, in spite of the fact that my teeth stick out from having stopped sucking my thumb only six years ago.

On the bus last month, I happened to sit across the aisle from a girl with pasty white skin and pale eyes lined in some kind of indigo gunk. We were right at the front, near the driver. The bus was so full there was no escape. She kept smiling like she had an imaginary friend. Every so often she'd lean forward and go, "Phe-ew," breathing right on me. The woman beside me wanted the whole bench to herself and edged me over with her enormous thighs until I was flattened against the metal railing. (I can't stand older women who wear stockings rolled, like floppy little doughnuts, down to their ankles.) She then took the shopping bag from her lap and mashed it between her ankles and mine as a further precaution that I wouldn't take up any more room than I had coming to me. Hot, numb with misery, and totally grossed-out, I closed my eyes and lost track of time. I went six extra stops and was fifteen minutes late for my appointment.

The old lady who runs the orthodontist's office also seems to run Dr. Fineman, who only appears, molelike, to run his fingers along your gums and then scurries off to other patients in other rooms. This old lady doesn't like kids unless they are with a parent. The first few months I went with my mother. Mrs. G. Blahuta, Receptionist (that's the sign on this dinosaur's desk) smiled and told me what a brave boy I was. She even exchanged recipes with my mother. That was four years ago. This past time, when I arrived late and gasping because I'm slightly asthmatic, Mrs. Blahuta (the orthodontist calls her Gladys; she has purple hair) scowled and asked me to come to the desk where I stood, wishing I could die, while she shrilled at me about inconsiderate teenagers who think of no one but themselves and show so little responsibility and motivation it's a wonder they can dress themselves in the morning.

Shaking with humiliation, I sat down to wait my turn beside a blonde girl with gold hairs on her beautiful tanned legs. She had been pretending to read a glamour magazine. Her eyebrows shot up as I sat down. She primly inched away and gave me her back like she was a cat and I was some kind of bug she couldn't even be bothered to tease.

On the trip home another gorgeous pristine-type girl swayed onto the bus two stops after mine. She sat down in the empty seat in front of me and opened the window I'd been too weak from my previous ordeals to tackle. This life-saving breeze hit my face, along with the sweet stirring scent of her musky perfume. Gratefully I watched the back of her neck. (She wore her hair up. The backs of girls' necks make me crazy.)

After about five more stops a sandy-haired man, whose stomach rolled like a pumpkin over the belt of his green work pants, got on the bus and sat down beside this breath-stopping girl. She didn't even seem to know he was there, and with great interest stretched her long neck to get a close look at a passing semi-trailer loaded with pigs. Their moist snouts poked at whatever air they could get at and you could tell they were on their way to the slaughterhouse. (Why else would pigs be spending a day in the city?)

The sandy-haired man readjusted his cap that was almost too small for his very large head. "Look at all them sausages!" he exclaimed, laughing really loudly at his dumb joke. The girl kept right on looking at the pigs. I could have died for her, but except for her nostrils that flared delicately and her slightly stiffened neck and shoulders, she didn't appear to be bothered at all.

The man playfully nudged her. "Hey!" he chortled, in a

voice that could be heard all over the bus, "You like pork chops?"

She turned from the pigs (I noticed her incredibly long eyelashes that were light at the tips) and stared straight at him. His face went into a silly fixed smile. "Excuse me," she said coolly, and got up to leave.

"Oh, your stop comin' up, little lady?" he bellowed as he got up quickly. Pulling at his cap brim, he let her past.

She walked about four steps down the aisle and moved in beside an expensively dressed Chinese lady with bifocals who looked suspiciously back at us, then frowned. I frowned at the fat man so she'd know it had been him, and not me, causing all the commotion.

I couldn't believe it when the man, calling more attention to himself, leaned forward and poked at a business-type suit person! He said, in what possibly for him was a whisper, "Guess she don't like pigs." The suit person gave him a pained over-the-shoulder smile.

The man finally settled back. "I used to live on a farm. Yup. I did. I really did," he continued to nobody in particular because everybody near was pretending to look out of windows, or read, or be very concerned with what time their watches gave.

"Whew! It's hot!" He all of a sudden got up and reached over the suit person, ruffling his hair. "Oh sorry," he said. "Mind if I open this?" He tugged open the suit's window. The suit shot him a look that suggested he wasn't dealing with a full deck. Which he probably wasn't.

I prayed he would leave but ten minutes later the girl of my dreams got off the bus. I was left staring at the pork chop man's thick, freckled neck.

His stop wasn't until one before mine. As we pulled away I watched him walk over and strike up a conversation with another complete stranger who was too polite to ignore him.

Like I said, you have to put up with some very weird people when you take the bus.

Today, I pleaded with my mother to drive me downtown. She lay on the couch popping painkillers because yesterday she fell and twisted an ankle and suffered a very small fracture as well. She isn't in a cast or anything and it's her left foot so she doesn't need it to drive with. When I asked her nicely for the second time, explaining that she wouldn't even have to get out of the car, she glared at me a moment and burst into tears. I don't understand why she's so selfish. I hope she gets a migraine from watching soap operas all day.

Can you believe it? I was late again for my appointment. I tried to explain to the purple-haired dinosaur that I'd missed my bus on account of being kept late in science class. (I had to re-write a test I'd messed up the first time because I was away sick the day the teacher told us to study for it and my friend Gordon, the jerk, was supposed to tell me and forgot to.)

Mrs. Blahuta said snidely that she was surprised I was only twenty minutes late and did I intend to put in an appearance at my next monthly appointment or would they all be kept in suspense until the final moment of the working day which was five o'clock. Sharp!

She kept me until every last person, except myself, had been checked over. At five to five she ushered me into the orthodontist as his last appointment for the day. He processed me as if I were some dog in a laboratory and then Gladys dismissed me by holding out my next month's appointment slip like it was a bone I'd probably bury.

I got out onto the street, saw my bus departing, and made a silent vow that for at least a month I wasn't going to speak to any person over the age of eighteen.

At five twenty-two I boarded my bus and all the seats were taken. As we got underway, I suddenly felt sick. I clung to the nearest pole while the bus lurched, braked, accelerated, and picked up three or four passengers at every stop. Heated bodies armed with parcels, babies, books, and briefcases pressed past me. Into his microphone, the driver ordered everyone to the back. I didn't budge. When his voice began to sound as if it were coming from inside a vacuum cleaner, another wave of nausea overcame me and my hands, hot and wet, slipped down the pole.

I hate getting motion-sickness. I'm sometimes so sensitive that just looking at, say, a movie of people going fast in a roller coaster can almost make me lose my last meal. Whenever I'm sick in the car, Mom says, "Fix your eyes on objects that are the furthest away. Don't look at anything that'll pass you by."

Remembering that, I turned to face the front of the bus. The furthest thing in my view was the pork chop man. As he was coming straight towards me, I shifted my gaze past his shoulder to a spot of blue that was, I guess, the sky. The bus took another shift and the sudden lurch swung me quickly around to where I'd been. I very nearly lost my battle with nausea to the skirts of a person wearing purple paisley.

Somebody gripped my arm, and said, "One of youse has to get up. This boy's going to be sick."

Immediately two people vacated their seats. Next thing I knew I was sitting beside a window with the pork chop man. He reached around behind me and tugged until wind hit my face.

"Hang your head out, now," he roared. "If you have to puke your guts out just go ahead and don't be shy." He patted my back in a fatherly way with one enormous hand while the other hung like a grizzly paw along the back end of my seat.

I did as I was told, breathed deeply for several seconds, and brought my head back in to have a look at him. I don't think I've ever seen such an enormous man. Up close, I realized he wasn't really so much fat as there was just an awful lot of him. "Name's Earl," he said, solemnly.

"Thanks, Earl," I said. "I'm Andrew."

"Don't have to thank me, Andrew. I joined A.A. two years ago. Haven't touched a drop since. I remember how it felt to be real sick."

I wanted to explain that I wasn't a drinker, but was overcome by another terrible feeling that I might lose control. Earl said, "Hold on, kid," and shoved my head out the window again.

We didn't talk much after that. It wasn't until my stop was coming up that I realized he'd just missed his.

I pulled the buzzer cord and said, "You missed your stop."

"How'd you know that?"

"I noticed you when you were on the bus one other time," I mumbled, embarrassed.

Earl sat back and looked straight ahead. He looked like a man who'd been struck by a thought that was almost too big to handle.

The bus arrived at my stop and Earl hurriedly got to his feet to let me past. I stepped off the bus with him right behind. On the street he said, still amazed, "You noticed me?"

The bus fumed noisily on past us.

"Yeah. Well—there was this girl, first. You came and sat beside her..." I trailed off.

"You know," said Earl, "just between you and me, city people aren't friendly. They don't notice nothing. See that old lady, there?"

At the light, an old girl tottered off the curb and started to cross the street. She carried two plastic Safeway bags full of groceries.

Out of the corner of his mouth, in a lisping whisper, Earl informed me, "If she was to fall and hurt herself just enough so she could still walk, not one person would stop and offer to help her home with those bags."

"That's true," I said, thinking that if they did, they'd probably turn around and help themselves to her purse.

We started across the street. I felt better, now that we were off the bus. I actually started to feel a little hungry. I wondered how I was going to say goodbye to Earl. I was afraid he might want to talk to me for a long time. He walked slowly and I felt obliged to keep pace with him.

We reached the other side and stopped on the sidewalk. All the while he kept going on about the time he'd taken some guy to emergency at the General Hospital. The guy had almost bled to death before they could get anybody's attention.

Without hardly pausing to breathe, Earl cornered me with his desperately lonely eyes and launched into another story. I made out like I was really interested but to tell the truth I was thinking about my favourite T.V. program, which would be on at that very moment, and about how Mom sits with me on the sofa, sometimes, while we eat our dinner and watch it together.

"Well," said Earl, too heartily, "I can see that you're going to be okay and I shouldn't keep you. Probably missed your supper, eh?"

He stuck out his hand, that massive freckled paw. Surprised, I took it and it surrounded mine in an amazingly gentle way. "Thanks," I said again.

"Told you not to mention it," said Earl. "We've all got to help each other out, don't we, buddy? But I can see I don't have to tell you that. You're different. You notice things."

In Orbit

Marie, there's this Orbit trash can. On Highway 23, just before you get to a place where they used to have a T.B. sanatorium, there it is. White. Like all the others the government put up along the roads for people to put garbage in. Those big round cans sure have been around a long time—I think maybe even before 1971, when I was not much older than you and just another scared kid off the reserve.

Anyway, that Orbit can on Highway 23 has a real special memory for your mama. So listen up good because it's going to take a bit of telling to get to that part of the story.

Mrs. Sidaway was a fat divorced white lady and the first person I saw when I stepped off the Grey Goose bus that comes from the city and before that from the Little Dog River Reserve. Mrs. Sidaway, she took me to a building that wasn't new but pretty, like old-time pictures of English cottages. Other native girls stayed there and I was given a room with Celeste Fontaine, who told me that behind her fat back everybody called Mrs. Sidaway, "Mrs. Sideways."

Mrs. Sideways was there to be a kind of watchdog and to teach us grooming and manners, like how you should change to a fresh pair of panties every day of the week, if

you own that many, and to always be polite to old people.
These things I already knew and so do you, Marie, because
I've taught you.

The sanatorium had once been used just for people with
tuberculosis. By 1971, doctors had got so smart about cur-
ing the disease they'd just about put themselves out of business. So the bigwigs from the city, who ran the place, got
the bright idea to ship kids just off the reserve there for some
months of upgrading and what they called "social skills"
before we were let loose on the big bad city. We were all
called "Socially Disadvantaged," and being at this special
school was supposed to change our lives for the better.

Celeste, she knew her way around that sanatorium pretty
good. In fact, she had a great-granny there, in the big infirmary, who was real sick with T.B. Back on the reserve, the
old lady had smoked a pipe all the time. Hardly ever took
it out of her mouth except to eat and sleep. So everybody
thought what she had was bad smoker's cough. One day
she coughed up a basinful of blood, and that's how they
found out she had T.B.

It was from visiting Celeste's great-granny that I met Elvis
Flett, whose mother must have been very musical. I only
called him Elvis at first, though. Later on I called him "Tomcat." Celeste's boyfriend, Harry Spence, was taking upgrading too. She got to see him all the time. With Elvis Flett it
was different. Like Celeste's granny, he had T.B. lungs—
though he wasn't as sick—so he couldn't do any old thing
he pleased. He had to stay in bed most of the time except
for meals, which were in another building, and for walks
that they let him take after he ate.

Elvis wore his hair down to his shoulders, like black shiny
crow wings, and his friendly brown eyes made you feel dancing as a creek when winter melts away.

The first time I saw him, he was standing outside his room
looking pretty strange with his Indian hair and his pale blue
white-man's pyjamas. But he was so handsome, I forgot
about the pyjamas and almost died from excitement. I poked
Celeste and she poked me back. We laughed. We couldn't

stop. All the time, Elvis Tomcat Flett stood in the hallway, tall and slender-bright, a springtime smile warming his face and opening me up where I never before knew I was closed.

Celeste, she shoved me towards him. "She likes your pyjamas," she said. We laughed all the harder. Tomcat gently tucked his hand under my arm to keep me standing up.

"We better go now," Celeste said, and she snorted and gasped. Her shoulders shook.

As we made our way down the hall, holding onto the walls, Tomcat called, "I got a green pair too!" and we just about fell over.

Every day for the next two weeks we went to visit Celeste's granny, but we didn't see Elvis outside his room again.

Celeste's granny. A little old lady with hair mostly grey, all done nice and neat by the nurses into one thick braid. So small in her bed, with bones that looked like they might break if you turned her over too fast. And every time she begged us to bring her a pipe. She was dying, you could tell, but somewhere back in her eyes was who she once was—a young girl, maybe like us. Did she wear two braids then? Did she love a slender boy? I couldn't understand why they wouldn't let her smoke since T.B. was killing her anyway.

We brought her licorice whips instead. She coughed and chewed at them just like a little kid. In a deep whisper, like wind rattling cottonwoods, she told us stories about the old people. By that time, in her mind I think they were still around and she was part of them. She made me hear long-ago drums. She said that death was right behind her shoulder, dusty, red-eyed, and he was a buffalo. Sometimes she looked sad.

One June day, outside the residence, we picked yellow roses from a big sunny bush. We thought they might cheer her up a bit. I stuck one in my hair, right behind my ear, in case I saw Elvis Flett, and Mrs. Sideways came out of her little office. You could always hear her before you saw her because her nylons made scratching sounds from her legs being too fat at the tops. She asked me, "Charlotte, what do you think you're doing?'' even though she wasn't blind. The rose from behind my ear did a summersault down my sweater and into my hand, the one without the roses.

"You can't pick them," said Mrs. Sideways. "We've waited all spring for those roses to bloom. Everybody wants to enjoy them.''

She smiled at me then as if she all of a sudden remembered she was talking to somebody who didn't know any better.

Celeste said, "My granny would like to enjoy them but she don't see too good from the infirmary.''

"How *is* your grandmother," said Mrs. Sideways, polite as a queen but not really asking.

"She's gonna die," said Celeste, with a mean look.

Mrs. Sideways gave a big sigh that made her bosoms flop around. "Take her the flowers, then," she said. Mrs. Sideways was the unjolliest fat person I ever met.

The day we took Celeste's granny the roses, I finally got up enough courage to knock on Elvis's door and ask if he ever went for walks with people that weren't patients. He seemed real happy to see me. From his bed he smiled like he was Adam and I was Eve and then he asked if I'd ever been up along Highway 23.

"I didn't know they let you walk that far," I said, hanging onto Celeste because I didn't want him to see me practically jump up and down.

"It's not that far," he said, kind of shy, and we all just hung around and smiled like our faces would fall off until Celeste finally pulled me out of the door. "Wait!" I hollered. "When?"

"After supper," he called back, sweet and quick, "near where the bus stops.''

Nowadays, you just stick your nose in an Orbit trash can and the flies'll carry you off. In 1971, Marie, the year of which I am speaking, they were as clean as a kid's playground. Cleaner than the highway. Or the ditches, for that matter.

It was Celeste who first got the idea to climb inside.

We were all walking along. My hand, in Elvis's, was a little puddle of hot skin and rubber bones. Celeste, she said to Harry Spence, "Know how white kids are always trying to see how many of them'll fit inside a phone booth?"

Harry was nice but kind of dumb. He couldn't remember anything about that.

"Or Volkswagen bugs," Elvis piped up. "They like to get jammed up inside little stuff."

"Right!" said Celeste. "So here's a question. How many Indians can you get inside an Orbit trash can?"

Harry said, "I give up."

Celeste rolled her eyes. "*Think,* Harry." Harry could really drive you crazy. "That can there is as little as it gets."

"So how many you figure?" said Elvis, looking at my face like it was the moon rising over a mountain.

Celeste grinned, then slipped through the round dark opening of the Orbit can. Disappeared neat and slick as a magician. "Come on, Harry, let's try for two," she called, hollow-sounding from inside. "It's just like a tiny space ship."

Harry shrugged, crawled in after her. He lit up a cigarette.

Smoke came out of the hole. Elvis made a joke about smoke signals from outer space.

Celeste and Harry giggled and wouldn't talk to us. Finally Elvis picked me up in his smooth strong arms and stuck me, feet first, after them. Harry's cigarette burned a hole in my jeans and we proved that three Indians can fit inside an Orbit can.

But two is best. And while Elvis Tomcat Flett and I were inside peeking out at the near full moon and the millions of prairie stars trailing light up the sky, Celeste's granny was back in the infirmary in her too-big bed where she'd just died all alone.

After that night I thought about how maybe her spirit flew up over Highway 23 to say goodbye to us. I wondered if as she hung overhead she wished she could have shared Harry's smoke. Or if she saw Tomcat kiss me inside the Orbit and ask me to be his woman.

It all happened a very long time ago, Marie. It's still a mystery in my life that night—Celeste and Harry and Tomcat and me all having fun while she was dying. But then maybe she would have wanted it that way. I don't know. Some memories are so strong and sweet and sad they seem to have a life of their own.

Waiting for the Carollers

M y parents called me Naomi because they both liked the name. I think that's the last thing they ever agreed on.

December twenty-first, I got on a jet plane heading west, with a stopover in Calgary. My destination: Kelowna, British Columbia, because that's where my grandmother lives. Her daughter, that's my mother, saw me off at the airport. Dad couldn't come because of a business meeting, he said. I know it's because he wasn't in total agreement with my going.

I wasn't in total agreement with my going.

Christmas can be a real bummer for some people. I know the ads all tell you how it's terrific and everything. But people starve to death at Christmas. Bombs go off. Countries are overthrown. Sick people get sicker and die. Some healthy people take guns and shoot themselves. Others feel disappointed because they didn't get what they wanted, or the family get-together was messed up by everyone fighting, or somebody got drunk, or somebody got really sick with the flu, or all of the above.

Christmas, for me, has never been an especially joyous occasion. I mean, what's left after they've told you there isn't a Santa Claus?

I'll bet even Jesus Christ Himself was sometimes depressed at Christmas.

My grandmother is retired. Grandpa died three years ago. Grandma makes pottery in the winter. In summer she sells peaches from her peach trees. When I say she's retired I mean that my grandparents moved to Kelowna when *he* retired so that makes Grandma sort of retired too.

No wonder Mom and Dad have never really gotten along. They met coming from opposite directions. Mom's dad was a zoology professor who spent his spare time fighting for world peace. Dad's dad worked for an insurance company and spent his spare time trying to improve his golf score.

Mom and Dad each came to their marriage expecting certain things. For one: that life together would be the happy idealized version each had of their own childhood home lives. They still expect it. They seem moronically unable to learn that you can't expect one person to give you all the things you want and need. Sometimes you just have to make do. God knows, I'm always making do. I don't get what I need, forget about what I might want.

I've learned that wanting is wishing your best friend would stop borrowing your clothes and never returning them. Or that you had more talent at something you work very hard at, when somebody else has talent to burn and lets it lay waste.

Needing is a different thing altogether. It's wishing for love with pennies at a dried-up well. Or waiting for family peace when home is an endless war zone.

My sister Sally says Mom and Dad will never change and she's just had to come to terms with that so why can't I. It's all very well for her to talk. Fact: she came to terms four years ago (at the ripe old age of nineteen) by getting married and moving out.

My brother Victor, who's older than Sally, remembers a time when Mom and Dad liked each other—or seemed to— and actually made jokes about how little they have in common. By the time I came along I guess it wasn't a joke anymore. I was one of the jokes they couldn't joke about.

Anyway, Mom's shipped me off to Grandma's for a boring festive season. She and Dad'll stay home and fight without me. I'm supposedly Grandma's Christmas present. Her *Christmas present,* can you believe it? I should have gotten off the plane wearing a goddamn bow around my neck.

I have to explain about my grandmother. She's seventy-five, short, rosy, and healthy (on account of she walks six miles every day whether or not she feels like it), goes to church regularly, is an NDPer (a bloody communist, Dad says) and *she does not live alone!* She's "Living in Sin" (Dad's expression) with a man who's four years younger than her. Edgar LaChance is his name.

Good old take-a-chance Edgar has a wife who, Grandma says, is in practically a vegetable state in a Kelowna nursing home. He visits her every Tuesday and likely lies about how swell everything is back home. Not that she cares, since she's a vegetable. He could tell her the entire West Coast was slowly sinking into the Pacific Ocean and she'd probably just lie there and drool.

Grandma lives on the other side of the lake from town, part way up what everybody here calls a mountain. For somebody who's supposedly a communist, she lives pretty well. The house overlooks the orchard (you can get a lot of peach trees onto one and half acres of land) and is all natural cedar with a huge fireplace smack dab in the middle. The mantlepiece is about a foot thick and this morning Grandma set Edgar and me to the job of decorating it, while she rushed off to find a freshly killed turkey as she refuses to buy a frozen one at the grocery store. They're shot clear through with chemicals, she says.

This afternoon, being Tuesday—can you believe this?—we are all going over to the nursing home to have a pre-Christmas celebration with Edgar's wife. I can't imagine anything more festive and jolly than that.

I'm even supposed to take her a present. Grandma bought Lily-of-the-Valley bath salts for me to take. I don't know how Edgar is going to introduce me. Am I the granddaughter of the woman he's living with? Who is his friend? Or his next-door neighbour? I don't even know if this old lady has met my grandmother. I also have a hard time visualizing how a vegetable relates to people. Does she blink her eyes— once for yes, twice for no?

Edgar and I lay cedar boughs on the mantlepiece. From a kicked-around looking cardboard box he eases out a Nativity scene, an old plastic crèche all in one piece with an electric cord dangling down the back. It's exactly the kind of gaudy thing a little kid would pick out to give to somebody special at Christmas. Plastic. My grandmother has always hated plastic. Once when I came to visit, she threw out my blue and pink barrettes and bought me brown ones that I didn't like as much. "But these are plastic too," I said.

"Tortoise-shell," she corrected me, even though she knew perfectly well they were plain old plastic.

Edgar's hands are dry as leaves. The backs are spotty with age marks and his veins are raised and ropey. He places the crèche at one end of the mantelpiece. Carefully he arranges cedar around it, then plugs it in. The little bulb inside comes on and lights up the Nativity scene. I choose that moment to ask what's wrong with his wife.

"Many things," he says, not taking his eyes off the crèche. He has a slight French accent.

I patiently wait for him to elaborate.

But Edgar isn't exactly a talker. In this he is unlike my grandmother who, when she opens her mouth, doesn't close it for a long time. Edgar watches her face whenever she talks, reviews it like it's a map: her eyebrows, eyes, nose, mouth, chin, and back on up again. Carefully he watches and, at the same time, seems to be thinking his own thoughts. He listens to CBC all the time and gets the same kind of look when he lifts his head from whatever he's doing to listen to certain passages of classical music.

My grandmother returns from shopping, her arms loaded with groceries she didn't intend to buy. Edgar takes them from her, sets them down in the kitchen. She removes her coat and hiking boots and pats her hair, which is always falling out of a loose French twist.

Edgar and I unload a few groceries. I toss a litre of Pecan Crunch ice cream into the freezer and, being in close proximity to freshly baked butter tarts, nip off the side of one and sneak it into my mouth.

"Not a fair test, one little piece," says Edgar, suddenly appearing at my shoulder. "Isn't it your duty, Naomi, to sweeten your tongue with the whole thing?"

Sweet filling encased in rich, salty pastry. Wiping away tell-tale crumbs, I follow Edgar into the living-room, where Grandma stands looking at the crèche.

"You found the turkey," says Edgar, kissing her cheek.

She nods. "They were dreadfully expensive, though. Oh Edgar!" she says, enraptured. "The crèche looks beautiful!"

I can't believe I'm hearing this.

She leans her head back against his green cardigan sweater. Cashmere. Edgar's a retired business executive from Montreal.

The thought has never before occurred to me, but I guess old people can fall in love. In all this time I've never seen her look peaceful. Happy, yes. Active. Excited. In charge. But never peaceful, like now.

It's a nice moment, just standing around beside them admiring that plastic crèche. Then my grandmother breaks the mood. She sets her shoulders, pushes up her sleeves, and says, "Well, let's have lunch. Then we'll go see Vivienne."

The first thing I notice about the nursing home is that it smells depressingly of baby powder. Next thing, that practically everybody there is in a wheelchair. A bunch of old people, all lined up in the big lounge off the rotunda. Like they're waiting for something. Nurses aides in pale blue uniforms keep wheeling more old people into the lounge. The lady at the front desk tells us that a choir is arriving soon to sing Christmas carols.

One of the walking residents is shuffling around holding a looped-over leather belt up to his mouth. One hand is in his pocket. He stops, turns to the wall, rocks back on his heels, and talks to his belt as if it's a microphone. He makes several announcements, loudly, importantly, in Ukrainian. The others pay him no notice. Like he's normal, for God's sake.

I want to turn around and walk back out. I've never felt so depressed in all my life.

Edgar says softly, "There's Vivienne."

I don't know what I expected Vivienne to look like. I guess totally grotesque. So I'm unprepared for this beautiful old lady. Her fluffy white hair is piled on her head. She's very European-looking. She wears art-type dangling earrings that must have been custom-designed for her. Her eyes are large, soft, greenish-blue. She has long, elegant fingers; the nails are short, unpolished and perfectly groomed, as if someone has done them for her.

"She used to be an artist," Grandma whispers to me. "She was famous, in a relative way. Their daughter died when she was quite young."

When who was young? Vivienne? The daughter?

Edgar crouches beside her wheelchair. He takes her hand and says something in French. She looks at his hand holding hers. He introduces us. I'm too busy watching her face to concentrate on what he's saying. It's the strangest face— beautiful, yes, but with no expression. No recognition.

Edgar hurries to the back of the room and returns with three metal fold-up chairs. He sets them down and then we all take seats, around Vivienne. From his breast pocket Edgar removes a small leather case, unzips it, and folds it out flat on the little table affair that is attached to the arms of the wheelchair. It's a manicure set. He begins to do Vivienne's nails, all the time talking to her, sometimes in French, sometimes in English. He tells her little jokes. He chuckles and smiles, all the while gently filing away at her pink perfect nails.

In ten minutes he says more than I've heard him say in the two days I've known him. My grandmother sits with her hands folded in her lap, saying nothing.

I guess people do what they have to do to get by. But Edgar amazes me. He does it so well, as if it hardly causes him any pain at all to be here in this place with his strange beautiful wife who was once an artist. Filing her nails is all that is left of their life together. Yet he does it with the greatest amount of love.

I feel my grandmother's hand along the back of my neck. Slowly, rhythmically, she begins to play with my hair. We sit in silence and wait for the carollers.

Like Lauren Bacall

Hollyhocks along our grandmother's back lane fence at the edge of town, pink and burgundy, with petals crisp as taffeta skirts. My cousin Avery with a pocketful of white stones. At nine years of age, he avoided stepping on ants and was an accomplished liar.

Under a six-foot tall hollyhock, he carefully counted his stones, setting them down like teeth against the deeply rutted lane. "I'm going to be a minister," he said, counting them out to twelve, one for every disciple. It was Sunday after church. "When I grow up I'll give long speeches and everyone will line up for bread and bloody wine."

"Bloody is a swear," I said, demurely smoothing my skirt with pudgy fingers.

"Bloody, bloody, bloody," he countered evenly, "is not a swear. Leg isn't a swear. Hand isn't a swear."

"Ministers don't swear and you're a liar. So you can't be one."

Little sour beads of sweat stood up on his mushroom cap nose. He lifted dark blue eyes, swallowing me up with his terrible magic, and pronounced, "You can't be a dancer because your name is Donalda. Nobody named that could be famous. I never ever heard of it before."

"I'll change my name to Nancy," I said desperately as his curls, chestnut brown like mine, bent once more over the stones. "And someday I'll be thin as a shadow, and then I'll go to Paris and dance with Gene Kelly."

"You'll never be a dancer," he shook his head solemnly, "Never, never, never."

I slapped my dirty red sandals all over his stones. I sent them scattering. He stood, momentarily taunting me with his beauty, then made a breathtaking cartwheel and hopped away on one foot. I followed him. I would have followed him anywhere. Even under a bus, if he'd asked me.

Seven years later, just before the summer of 1960, I acquired a driver's license and access to the family car, and with the help of a case of chocolate-flavoured Metracal shed twenty-three pounds and became a glamour girl. I took up smoking and bought a black linen dress, cinched at the waist with a patent leather belt. The deep V down the back showed off my tan like pictures you see of starlets in movie magazines. And, further to that end, I French-inhaled and wore my hair seductively slanted over one eye, like Lauren Bacall.

I was attracted to fast cars and dangerous boys and when I got off the bus at Lumley, B.C., I flirted outrageously with the bus driver, the only decent-looking male on board during the whole dreary ride across two dusty provinces. Appreciatively, he watched my legs as I descended the steel-tread steps. He took my hand to help me from the final step to the ground. Over his shoulder, framed inside the bus depot doorway and looking like a Norman Rockwell painting, was my grandmother—a tall, china-cup lady in a lilac cotton dress. She smiled as if the sun had just come out, and slowly waved. I had expected Avery to meet me. He was nowhere in sight.

I was raised in a small Saskatchewan town, and Lumley was five times the size of what I had left behind. My parents, however, had been to Europe—a distinction that I felt, at least by association, gave me a certain worldly sophistication. I was confident in my new clothes. Everything was as it should be. Furthermore, I had decided ahead of time that the seven years since my last visit would have brought little change to Grandma's sprawling town. In my imagination I'd vividly recalled abundant apple orchards, nearby Marion Lake—cool and spring-fed—and the park two blocks from her house. Nothing in this tranquil picture, with the exception of Avery and me, would have changed.

In the summer of 1953, lady shoppers stopped my grandmother on the streets of Lumley to ask if Avery and I were twins. We were the same height, and although I was overweight, our features were remarkably alike. There, however, all likeness ended. He was the cousin who could do anything: shinny barefoot up a telephone pole, stand on his hands in Marion Lake and never get water up his nose, have all the neighbourhood kids believing he was actually a Martian orphan with strange alien powers. He could also tell our grandmother almost any lie he pleased and she'd believe him. When a neighbour hesitantly informed her that her child's doll had been stolen, its private parts garishly decorated with red nail polish, then secretly returned, and that all the children were saying Avery had done it, Grandma primly replied, "That doesn't sound a bit like Avery and I can't imagine where he'd get nail polish."

Grandma's nails were pristine moons set into scrubbed tanned flesh. She was delicate, fearless, seventy-four, and had been widowed by my flamboyant, loving grandfather when Avery was seven. Together, Grandma and Grandpa had raised five children of their own and had taken on Avery with very little discussion or fuss in the summer of 1944, when their youngest son was blown up by the Germans on the coast of Normandy and their daughter-in-law decided she couldn't handle motherhood and widowhood at the same time.

Gram didn't own a car. We walked the five blocks from the bus depot to her house, passing the park along our way. "It has a public swimming pool now, Doni," she informed me with civic pride. "Built last year by the Kiwanis. Avery has a summer job there. I hope you brought your bathing suit."

His summer job, predictably, was as a lifeguard. But that's not where I saw him for the first time in seven years.

"He wanted to meet you," said Grandma, and my spirits lifted. "He's so busy now, with his job. You'll see him soon. He's off duty at two today." Soon I set down my suitcase inside her cool house, inside the freshly painted kitchen with its remembered shelves and knick-knacks.

On a yellow shelf by the window, a plaster bluebird, painted badly by a childish hand, rested beside a small brass teapot. It was the same pot I'd made grass tea in one day, just outside the back lane fence. A neighbourhood girl and I were playing teaparty with our dolls. Avery wouldn't pretend to drink the tea and he wouldn't be the daddy. He just sullenly leaned against the fence, arms folded, and told us we were dumb girls. He pulled flowers off the hollyhocks and threw them in our hair. We screamed at him. He took off down the lane, stopped part way, and flipped over onto his hands. Suddenly his feet were dancing against clouds and sky. When I blinked my eyes in the hot white sun, he'd brought them down again and was already running past the gate three houses away.

I picked up the pot and cradled it in the palm of my hand (how small it was!) as Gram plugged in the electric kettle to make us real tea as we waited for Avery.

Her house was full of braided rugs and memories. I sat in her rocker, hugging a frayed pillow that was decorated with a handpainted picture of the Banff Springs Hotel. I watched her bring out two faded teacups and two blue-willow patterned plates and place them on the heavy oak kitchen table. A freshly baked pie sat on the metal shelf over the back burners of the wood-burning stove.

"You have a new stove, Gram," I said, pointing to the modest electric range across the room from the wood burner. The kettle bubbled and steamed. She pulled the plug, made the tea at the new range, then brought the teapot over to the old one. After setting it down, she raised a burner lid and poked with a black metal rod at the slow fire. She said, "I'm not quite used to that one yet. Avery gets quite impatient with me."

He didn't arrive home until away after dinner. Grandma and I had eaten the meal she'd made especially for my welcome. Baked chicken. Green beans from her garden. A raspberry custard pie, delicious and faintly smoky—Avery's favourite, apparently.

His dinner sat warming in the new stove, nestled under an inverted tin plate.

"I told him you'd be here and to come home early," said Grandma apologetically. "I'm sure he hasn't forgotten. But he's probably met up with some of his friends. He sometimes does that."

I'd been with her since one o'clock. We'd talked about the family and what all her neighbours were doing and the high cost of living. We'd toured her garden and I'd sampled enormous gooseberries and noted the tall, straight hollyhocks that still grew against the fence. We'd eaten dinner and "repaired" to the livingroom. There she'd picked up her crochet work, and I'd leafed through drab knitting books showing black and white pictures of babies in buntings, babies wearing sweater sets and hats with ribbons and strange clubfoot-looking booties, babies who were probably all grown up now and yelling at their own kids, but who in the pictures stayed grey and water-stained and forever smiling. I was becoming bored and I desperately needed a cigarette.

Finally we heard him. The back gate squeaked on unoiled hinges and banged loudly shut, and Grandma gave a little start, threw down her crochet work, and abruptly rose from her livingroom chair. I dashed to the hall mirror to make sure my lipstick was still fresh, my hair appropriately slanted over my left eye. Frantically, I smoothed the creases from my form-fitting black linen dress and then slinky, like a sloe-eyed cat, like a sultry Lauren Bacall, I slipped through the kitchen door to meet my cousin Avery.

He stood in the dim evening light by the back door, a much taller Avery dressed in crumpled chinos and a striped T-shirt. He was barefoot, tanned, very fit and handsome. I don't think, at first, he saw me.

Grandma didn't ask him why he'd been so late. She seemed only to care that he was home and shuffled on slippered feet from the stove to the table with his dinner plate.

He and I were no longer the same height. Even with me in my satiny black high heels, my eyes were level with his shoulders as I reached him, placed my hand on his arm—this stranger from my childhood—and said, "Hello." I didn't know what I should do next. Back in Saskatchewan I'd fantasized that my magical cousin would meet me at the bus. He'd get out of the car (his own, although I hadn't quite thought out how he would have managed that) and he'd lift me off the ground and comment on how much weight I'd lost and how beautiful I'd grown. And then we'd drive the long way through town to Grandma's, stopping at the café for a Coke, and everyone would stare at us and think how good we looked together, and just for a little while—without a word or a familial kiss on the cheek—we'd let them think that we weren't really cousins on the way to Grandma's, but lovers on our way to Marion Beach or to Vancouver or to see the world.

Avery jerked away, like someone startled awake from a good dream. He finally focused on me, said softly "Hi," and it was then I realized he was drunk. "They were cleaning out the pool today. I stayed to give them a hand, Gram."

"That's just like you, dear. Always helping out," said Grandma, at the counter. She cut into a large wedge of raspberry custard pie, transferred it to a plate, licked her fingers clean.

Slumping into a chair at the head of the kitchen table, Avery then began to wolf down his dinner. Wordlessly I joined him at the table and watched him eat. Grandma poured milk into an oversized glass. He took it, drank half, clumsily set it down. It fell over, and Grandma rushed to the sink to get a rag. Milk dripped from the plastic tablecloth down the imitation lace frill onto the black-and-white linoleum. Avery watched Gram, down on her hands and knees cleaning up, and when she carried the sopping rag away, he turned to me and said, "So. You're all grown up. How's good old Saskatchewan?"

I didn't reply. I left the table, went into the guest room, took a chic black cardigan out of my suitcase, and threw it casually over one shoulder. Without telling either of them where I was going, I slipped out into the cool Okanagan evening. I lit a cigarette on the front street, then my high heels tapped their own jazz down the sidewalk. By the time I'd reached the main street, my cigarette was low and I was high on nicotine. I found a Dairy Queen, so new the pink sunset reflected in the shiny clean paint. And a handsome boy pulled up to the window where I stood licking my cone, pulled up slick as silk in his father's dangerous dark blue convertible, got out and bought a cone, and stood with his back to the building, eyeing me before finally getting up the nerve to say, "Hi, where are you from?"

I gave him my shoulder with the deep V down my back, then slowly turned, smiled a Hollywood smile, and as I walked away, teased, "My name is Nancy. I study ballet in Paris, and I'm just passing through."

Dying for Love

I'm in love with Philip Chester. Oh, why couldn't I have been born a blonde? I have hair that looks like it's been soaked overnight in a coffee pot. And mud-green eyes. And, God how I hate them, freckles. I've tried Porcelana on these freckles. I've lain for hours with lemon slices on my face. I've delicately applied Revlon's Touch and Glow and worked over each of God's little sun-kisses with generous smears of cover-up stick, but nothing works.

I could bleach my hair but my mother won't let me until I'm an old maid. I'm saving up to buy some pearly sea-foam eyeshadow. I don't mind being tall or that my shoulders are broad; I look great in sweaters. But the freckles are hopeless. They were cute when I was six. What do I do now that I'm fourteen?

Philip Chester, whom I have loved from afar since I was in grade three and he was in grade five (I'm mad for his kisses and he's kissed more girls than a dog in June drops grey ticks), likes girls who are tiny-faced baby dolls.

Yesterday, I had no intention of sending the note I wrote in science class. Marti Panchuk (we call her Pancakes; her breasts are in an arrested state of growth) found it in the hall where it had dropped out of my notebook, and she *pinned it up on the school bulletin board* for everyone to see. Including Philip! Oh God, I wanted to die. If it had just been an ordinary love note. But oh no! Miss Blabbermouth of the Century had to tell him how much she'd like to get him alone and cover him with kisses, because he's so *sweet*—like a giant candy cane. We are talking megamortification here.

If I'd been Lucia di Lammermoor or Tosca or Madama Butterfly I could have fallen down, shrieking and stabbing myself, and that would have ended it. The tragedy of real life is that the prime causes of personal anguish are often hilarious to lookers-on. At the opera? All the world's great love themes get played out properly and people die horribly, slowly, and for the right reasons. Nobody laughs. There isn't a single real-life person anymore who's willing to die for love.

My mother's going through early menopause and I'm going through late puberty. She doesn't have freckles or wrinkles. I found her on her hands and knees on the floor when I came home from school. I was skipping last class because I could no longer tolerate my snickering classmates or the whole rest of Sandler Collegiate, where I am a low-life junior, as if that weren't in itself enough to cause me to jump off a bridge.

With a wet blue J-cloth and a broken fingernail, she flicked away splatters of dried-up fudge brownie batter from the kitchen floor-tiles. "I wish you would be neater in the kitchen," she sighed one of her sighs, then looked up as I stood there needing her to say something a little more relevant about my life. I screamed at her. I told her she was a shallow bitch. A blanked-out expression, and then a hot flush as she screwed up her pretty-as-a-flower face. She stood. "Ardis!" she screamed, "Go up to your room!"

"My pleasure," I said, and turned and went upstairs. I slammed into my room and dove, in tears, onto my navy-and-peach patchwork quilt. My fat old tabby cat bounced into the air from a sound sleep and squawked like a sat-on squeeze-toy as his feet hit the floor.

I have never in my life called my mother a bitch. I've just

thought it lots of times. She thinks she owns me. She doesn't like anything I like (except the opera). She yells at me for the slightest little thing. She nags. She lectures. She wants me to be perfect like she isn't.

Every other mother I know works at an important job. It's embarrassing to tell kids that my mother is a cheer lady every Thursday afternoon at the hospital, pushing around carts of peppermints and year-old magazines. She also volunteers Tuesdays on Palliative Care, where they put all the patients who are dying. Her favourite colour used to be peach. We even had a peach sofa and matching love seat. Now that she plays Florence Nightingale, she's passionate about leaf green. Says it's an Alive Colour. I won't let her touch my room. I hate green.

In the halls today, first thing as the hot morning sun shooed us off the street to scurry like rats to our classes, Lisa Malone caught up with me. Her quite small blue eyes sparkled maliciously. This is the third time she's talked to me this year. "God, I can't believe you wrote that to him," she burbled. "I wouldn'ta had the guts to do it. Whattid he say, anyways? I mean, he musta flipped." She blew a pink bubble and snapped it, backwards, into her gloss-sticky mouth.

"Lisa, your hair looks like something my cat regurgitated," I said, pushing past her for math class. Lisa, who has perfect hair (she keeps hair spray, mousse, gel, and a curling iron in her locker) looked stricken, then said, "Geez, Ardis. You don't have to take a major. Like, it isn't the end of your life or anything."

Then a miracle happened. Marti Pancakes passed me a note in math class. It said: "Don't feel bad. Phil really likes you. No kidding. Sorry about yesterday. Write back if we're still friends."

I've never been friends with Marti. Nobody's friends with Marti. She lives in the constant glow of romance (not her own, everyone else's). To be friends with her is to admit you're a total social washout. But I had to risk it so I could ask, "How do you know Phil really likes me?"

"Because he told me," said Marti, turning around, pushing

her fishy glasses back on her nose, blinking her bulgy carp eyes.

Phil is sixteen and the tallest boy in school. He hangs around with Bobby Ferreira and Gordon Field, who date the same type of girls as he does: blonde and perfect like Lisa. If Phil stands over you, when you can get close enough for that, the world falls away and you can't breathe. Not that you need to, much. What's so great about breathing anyway? The purest most beautiful notes in opera are surrounded by the rarified air of love and anguish, and I can hold my breath as long as any opera star alive. I've done it, sitting in the darkened concert hall, pierced to the heart while a note goes on and on and everyone else in the audience breathes and coughs.

The buzzer goes. I find my feet as Marti disappears in a crowd of heads, before I can get the chance to ask the whens and whats of Philip Chester liking me. She's keeping me hanging so I'll have to talk to her again. I'm jostled into the hallways, carried along by a stream of kids. Some leave the stream, swallowed up by their appointed classrooms; others flow into the stream. There is, as well, a stream coming from the other direction. I have to pass through that one, as do several people ahead of me. The streams converge in confusion. I struggle to the other side. Philip Chester is coming out of Science Lab. It must be an omen! People push past us. He takes my arm and gently steers me off to one side. I am dizzy. I may possibly faint. The top of my head comes as far as his open shirt collar. He smiles shyly and deliciously. His eyes are smoky blue. His dark brown hair falls over his forehead. I should be dying of embarrassment but instead I'm dying for love. He must be the sweetest boy in the universe. I don't know if I can hold my breath much longer.

Then, quietly breaking the spell and my heart, he says, "It was pretty funny what you wrote yesterday. Too bad you signed it. Pancakes will believe anything. I really blew up at her. It was a joke, eh Ardis?"

He doesn't mean to be cruel. He just is. He can't stand

it, what I wrote about him. He wants me to tell him, out loud, the six years of this feeling that has grown up inside me has been a lie.

At the kitchen table, Mom's scrunched over paper and figures. She keeps the accounts for Dad's printing business. I flop down into the chair across the table from her, books still in my arms. Without looking up from adding a column of figures, she says, "I'm making your favourite kind of chicken for supper. Do you want noodles or brown rice?"

"Doesn't matter," I shrug.

She looks up then, takes off her glasses, props them on her head. Parental radar scans my face for clues. "How's school?"

"All right," I push back on my chair. Lightly kick the table leg.

She watches me steadily. I don't tell her stuff. She used to try to drag it out of me. All I want is a hug. She wants a discussion.

She says, "I'm going over to Palliative Care tonight. Visiting someone who'd really cheer you up. Want to come?"

Doesn't matter.

On the way over to the hospital Mom is real quiet. She's trying to quit smoking. This is the fourth time she's tried. Our car smells fresher this past two weeks and the ashtray overflows with gum wrappers. With one hand she manoeuvers the steering wheel as the tires lick up the dark streets. Purse between her knees, she fumbles for gum and comes up with two squares of Fleer's Double-Bubble. "Want one?" she says, holding it out.

"Reverting, are we? Going through our second childhood?" I say, making an effort at gaiety so she won't keep stealing anxious looks at me. It works. She chuckles. When she's not in a state of menopausal hysteria, we can sometimes joke around.

I unwrap the gum and watch graceful black lamp-posts slip by. They're all along the river near the hospital, and are softened by imitation gaslights. They call this section of the street The Promenade, and the rich orangey lights and people casually sauntering along the riverside and near the old stone Roman Catholic cathedral make you feel as if you're caught in a time warp.

The hospital is run by nuns. There are crosses everywhere and God Loves You plaques. Religious fervour gives me the creeps. It's ten to nine, past the usual visiting hours. A security officer who's been sitting near the elevators, looking at his shoes, gets up and tells Mom she's not going any further unless she gets a pass. She produces a little red card, grandly flashes it at him. As if it were orchestrated, he backs off and at the same time some elevator doors open. We step inside. We're the only passengers. Mom leans back, folds her arms across her ulta-suede trench-coat, looks sidelong at me, and blows a bubble that immediately bursts.

The doors to all the rooms are posted with elongated signs in black vertical oriental lettering. "They say Welcome in Chinese," Mom explains. "One of the nurses is taking a course in calligraphy."

Beside the Chinese welcome on 528 is a small hanging basket of silk irises and tulips. The doors to most of the rooms are open. This one is partly closed. Mom raps lightly before hesitantly entering the room. It's occupied by two patients. A nurse in a white pantsuit and belted cardigan sweater pulls across a curtain between the beds. She adjusts the i.v. on the youngish woman who is closest to us and smiles distantly in our direction before she leaves the room. The dark-haired woman lies on her back. In a chair that is pulled right up beside her is a man. Like her, he is probably in his late twenties. His hair is too short, like he's just got it cut. We see him from the back; his ears are red, his head droops. Her hand on the bedspread almost touches his. She talks softly, though her eyes are closed.

Standing near the window, arms folded, looking out, is the patient I presume we've come to see. She turns, smiles when she sees it's us. She's tanned. An Arizona retiree-type grandmother with steel grey hair who looks too healthy to be dying. She wears a flowing mint-green satin gown over

the standard nondescript blue that's always too short even
if you're a midget.

We come together and whisper for a while, like three
worn-out geese in a deaf-making wind. The woman is a
smiler. Even her eyes smile. I feel as if I've know her all
my life. With both hands she touches my shoulders and tells
my mother I'm a beauty. Her name is Rachel.

With a kind of cautious grace she inches over to her bed,
sits on the edge. "I'm going home tomorrow, Ida," she says,
and softly enfolds her bare feet under the covers. "Just for
a few days. My son and my two grandchildren are coming
to collect me."

I get this mental picture of bits of Rachel spread all over
the room. The children pasting her together, giggling over
which pieces fit where. Setting her on a chaise longue.
Decorating her hair with purple irises and orange tulips.

"Rachel is an opera star," says my mother, out of the blue.
She nods and smiles at me, then at Rachel who smiles bril-
liantly back.

"Used to be," corrects Rachel. "That was a long time ago.
I still love my music." She plays with a heavy gold ring,
set with an enormous dark-coloured gem, on the fourth
finger of her right hand. "Your mother tells me you two
never miss the opera."

The young man abruptly appears from behind the curtain
separating Rachel and her neighbour. "I'm stepping out.
Going for a coffee," he interjects.

Rachel immediately lifts her head to him. "I'll listen for
her," she says.

He runs one hand over his inch-long hair, shoves the other
hand into his pocket, and without another word disappears.

Rachel smooths and folds the edge of her sheet. "Poor
things," she says gently. "She really isn't well at all. He's
here all the time. He must sleep on the couch in the coffee
room."

I think of Phil and how he waited impatiently for an
answer that would push me far away.

"I was just fooling around—I didn't mean it, any of it,"

I mumbled finally, and watched his shoulders slowly sag with relief.

"You've got to be careful," he said, smiling easily. "Can't go around putting things on paper you don't mean."

Rachel looks distractedly at her hands. Then, just as quickly, she's happy again. "I've been so lucky," she says. "In Chicago, thirty years ago, we opened in *La Traviata*, and I played Violetta." She raises her eyes, looks directly at me. "Are you familiar with *Traviata*, Ardis?"

I nod my head. I must not look away. Frail Violetta, ill with a fatal disease, sings her lungs out until Act IV and then dies, her grief-stricken lover at her bedside.

"Do you remember," Rachel continues evenly, "the meltingly beautiful love songs? Alfredo was played by a young tenor from Boston. What a voice! What a man!"

She startles me then with what I would never have expected to hear in this sad place: a voice such as hers, still beautiful. She sings, *"A quell'amor ch'e palpito, dell'universo intero..."* It's the best section of the best aria and you always have to wait three minutes for Violetta to finally get there. How could Rachel have known that, out of the whole opera, this is the place where I'd like to lie down and live forever, even though it lasts only a minute and forty-five seconds. She finishes and sighs. Mom sighs. I'm barely breathing. She says in English, "That love, the pulse of the whole world... mysterious, unattainable. The torment. And delight!" Even her laughter is musical. "And *delight* of my heart!" She sighs again, dramatically, playfully, and winks at me.

My mother, laughing, crying, reaches over and energetically pats my hand. Suddenly I feel absurdly happy.

For Mom and Rachel and me, time has stopped on a heartbeat. There is no before, no after. We aren't any age, yet we are all ages. And there is no death. Only us, each somebody's daughter, three conspirators on the battlefield of love.

Sunlight
Through Organdy

arly this morning I heard a meadowlark outside the bedroom window. His song reminded me of sunlight through organdy, of a long-forgotten curtain in another bedroom window.

The summer I turned seventeen, I was sent to work at a T.B. sanatorium as a ward aide. It was the thought of my parents that if I had a taste of boring, repetitive work, I might return enthusiastically in the fall to finish my high school education.

Mother trundled me off to the bus, my belongings in assorted mismatched suitcases and two cardboard boxes. One of these included curtains she had just finished making for my bedroom on the farm. They were of fine white organdy, painstakingly stitched together on her old treadle sewing machine.

"Put them up when you get there. You won't be so lonesome for home." She laid a damp cheek against mine. I drew back while her arm still clung. "Write," she said, studying me with wren-brown eyes. "I know you'll be a good girl."

Embarrassed, I boarded the bus and didn't once look back.

I intended to fill my sketch book in my spare hours; it had never entered my mind to be anything but good. Back in grade four I had been told by a teacher that poor students were often very creative. The better I became at drawing, the more clearly I could see how right she was.

Roxanne, a kitchen maid, roomed with me. I was summer help and she mistook me for an intellectual because I wore glasses and read books when I wasn't sketching. She was literal-minded and, lacking imagination, couldn't accept the correct way my mother had taught me to speak: "Why don't you talk English?" or the way I dressed: "Geez Lorraine, don't you wear any colours except white and blah-ck?" or my social life: "Too good to come out and drink a few beers with me and Morley, eh?" Morley was her boyfriend and an orderly in the infirmary. Roxanne was nineteen and had decided to make a career of being a kitchen maid until she married Morley.

She felt personally attacked the day I hesitantly took down the heavy mustard-yellow curtains that came with the room and replaced them with the silk-sheer organdy. Ready for combat, arms folded, she said, "So what was wrong with them yellow ones?"

I stared at the view past the curtains. Rain sagged down the glass and filled the room with a melancholy dampness. I kept my back to her, one hand pinning back a sheath of white organdy. Three stories below, balsams with branches slender as girls' arms edged the front road. Beyond, half-hidden from view, were the terraced lawns and formal gardens that were a showplace for dignitaries visiting the institution. And a thundery sky hung over the lake in the angry green distance.

I turned around in time to see Roxanne with an armful of perfectly folded yellow curtains, which she then shoved onto the top shelf of her clothes closet.

A week and a half after I arrived, a young intern caught my attention in the cafeteria by dropping his tray on my toes. He was slender, dark, and had what was then commonly termed x-ray eyes. He apologized by joining me at my table, where I'd gone to sit alone to eat my lunch and read *The Return of the Native*.

Book flat on the table, I hunched over and nibbled soda crackers instead of making them swim grotesquely in my turkey noodle soup.

"Thomas Hardy, well, well," he said, lifting the book to peer with restless curiosity at the title. "You like to read?"

"Yes," I said, immediately mistrusting him. "I like to read."

"What else do you like to do?"

I tried to ignore this while I read over the same sentence.

He sat back, sighed, drummed his fingers on the formica tabletop. I could feel his eyes on me, burning through me. He finally said, "How old are you?"

I looked up and flared, "Nineteen. And I prefer to eat alone." I had no reason to lie. But there it was, I'd gone and done it. Maybe it was his shoes, which were a thin, velvety leather.

"Go ahead," he said, lifting his foot, resting ankle on knee. The foot jogged up and down; the soles of his expensive shoes were barely worn. He said with a devastating smile, "I won't disturb you. I'll just watch."

I returned to my meal, but my hands began to tremble. Some soup dribbled down my chin.

He quickly reached over and swiped a serviette from the dispenser at the empty table beside us. Delicately he dabbed away the soup from my chin. "My name's Laurence Grant," he said, then added almost tenderly, "Would you like to go sailing with me—tonight, after work?"

I'd never been in a sailboat. It seemed the most glorious thing in the world would be to sail away, willy-nilly, anywhere the wind took you. So that evening, when Laurence asked where I would like to go, I couldn't think, just blurted, "The end of the lake?" and was surprised and flattered when he obliged me. The ride was shifting shimmering movement, tall white sails, luminous and foam-tipped waves, the sun all falling heat and flame. Orange light played over the water, along the beaches, and up the darkly treed hillsides. On the way back Laurence reached over and placed his hand lightly on my bare knee. His fingers were narrow and tapered at the tips, his skin ochre in the fading sunset. "Are you cold?" he asked.

"No," I replied, shivering. I began to roll down my pant-legs. Lazily, he withdrew his hand.

It wasn't that I was totally inexperienced. But I was used to the boys in the district where I'd lived all my life. Either they turned red just taking your hand, or they'd get you in a car, park somewhere, kiss you once, and try to slide you back down on the seat. None of them moved me. I kissed them because they expected it, all the while wondering what I was supposed to be feeling.

Laurence wasn't like them. He was a man. He wasn't in any particular hurry, which fascinated and terrified me. When he suggested we should go sailing the following Saturday, I agreed with an eagerness that made him smile and sent me home, shame-faced, to hide under my covers.

"You're dating Dr. Grant," said Roxanne, rolling her eyes. "*Dr.* Grant."

"We're going sailing," I replied defensively.

"Sailing," she repeated, her tone suggesting I'd just told her I was planning to rob a bank. "Well! Me and Morley are going to the drive-in and you can just stay behind and get yourself into hot water is all I can say. They don't like it, you know, when aides date doctors."

"Who doesn't?"

"Everybody. You'll get talked about and nobody'll talk to you."

I smiled. "Then that will be one less person than who talks to me now."

"Listen," Roxanne hissed, "don't think you're the only girl who's ever gone out with Dr. Grant in his sailboat."

"And what if they have?" I pouted. "I'm the one he wants to take now."

Roxanne snorted. "You'll find out. You can't come here, Miss Know-It-All, and put up fancy curtains and read fancy books and date doctors and go sailing. That's for rich people. You'd just better learn where you belong in life."

That was the most creative remark Roxanne had made to me. So I went sailing all day Saturday in high winds, got a blistering sunburn, and caught a summer cold that sent me to bed for the first three days of the following week. There I relived endlessly my sail with Laurence, who was absolutely the most sophisticated person I'd ever met. In his wallet he carried a photograph of his beautiful mother, who had been a cellist with the symphony orchestra before hanging herself, at the age of thirty-seven, when he was ten. He looked quite like her, with the same dark features, the same penetrating gaze. But hers was an almost madly gay smile that made the fine hairs along my arms suddenly stand on end. I handed him back the picture, face down. He caught my discomfort and said, "She was fun to be with. Especially summers at the lake. We captured minnows in tin pails. When she was well, people thought she was my father's daughter—not a wrinkle, very beautiful." There were no pictures of his father, a prominent Montreal physician, or his brother, now a journalist living in Paris.

Laurence himself had once been an accomplished cellist, but for three generations the eldest sons in the Grant family had been doctors. So now he played only occasionally. When he asked me about my family, what was I to say? That my father spoke broken English and my mother, an ex-primary school teacher, had worn the same dress to church for the past ten years? That my sister, who had been the hope of the family because she was so smart and pretty, had run off and gotten married when she was barely sixteen? Instead, I smiled mysteriously into the sun before returning my attention to my sketch pad. I had long before learned that the things people guess about you are far more interesting than any truth they could know.

At noon on the third day of my illness, Laurence appeared at the open door of my room. He leaned against the door frame, then tapped softly. I had felt his presence, like a shadow, before I actually saw him. His flapping white doctor's coat looked somehow misplaced against his elegant thinness, as if it were a theatrical prop and at any moment the real Laurence might appear. Rumpled, unshaven, smiling morosely, he waved a bouquet of zinnias. I was totally enchanted. He stepped into the room, into a pool of light. A small miracle, it seemed, come to rescue me. Stopping just short of my bed, he handed over the flowers at arms' length. He said, again with that smile, "You're such a child."

"I have a cold," I said gaily, making room for him to sit at the edge of the bed.

He went to the open window, where he stood looking into the distance. A warm wind caught the organdy curtains. They billowed out like twin kites.

"You have a cold," he said, lightly fingering the silken cloth, "because you want to avoid me. You're afraid of your emotions."

To my surprise he then turned, came to my bed, bent down, and kissed me. It was the sweetest, most mournful kiss—our first intimate contact since he'd touched my knee. I twined my arms around his neck, pulling him closer. Much too soon his hands were on my arms, tugging them away. Abruptly he stood over me, silent, angry, and then left with a confused, "Goodbye."

Disappointed, hurt, I waited an entire week before I stopped him on the ward where we both were working the same shift and confronted him. "We've gone sailing twice, you've brought me zinnias which you probably stole from one of the flower beds, and you've kissed me once. Is that all I get?"

He regarded me with horror, as if I'd dropped something unspeakable on the floor. "I have patients to see," he said. "Excuse me."

"Why?" I blocked his way. "If you can wipe soup off my face and touch my knee because you feel like it and leave me just when you've made the decision a kiss should end, then why can't I ask what's in all this for me?"

"I'm really very sorry," he said, fidgeting on the spot. "All I can say is...I never meant to hurt you."

"I certainly find that hard to believe."

"Lorraine, you're a nice prairie girl, raised on milk and oranges," he said slowly, avoiding my eyes. "We can be friends. That's all. If you like we'll still go sailing together."

"Thank you very much," I replied haughtily, "but I don't appreciate being the object of your whims. I'm not that lonely."

"Let me tell you a thing or two about our Dr. Grant," Roxanne announced later. She went to the window, opened it about a foot, pulled down the blind and shut out the setting summer sun.

"Leave it up," I said.

She shrugged and tugged the metal ring, and the blind noisily spun back to the top of the window. The organdy curtains seemed to catch fire. Outside, birds urgently trilled evening songs.

Roxanne came and flopped onto my bed where I sat, not bothering to remove my worn pink slippers. She wasn't unattractive, I decided, even in curlers, her unwashed hair secured with a net bandanna. She had cat's eyes, actually that shade of green, and lush naked lips. She continued, "The first time I saw Laurence Grant, I was sitting outside, minding my own beeswax, chomping a Oh Henry bar. He comes up and stands over me, hands on his hips, sleeves on his fancy dress shirt rolled up, and he says, 'So that's how you keep your voluptuous shape.' And he's smiling his piano-board smile. Like he's real hot stuff. Only thing is, Lorraine, that's what he does. Get it? That's *all* he ever does."

She shifted her position, seemed about to say something else and, instead, pursed her lips. I quickly looked down at my slippers, and began pulling out little withered tufts of pink fur.

She reached over and gently placed her hand on mine. "You'll make them bald," she said. "They're bad enough."

Then, uncertain for the first time since I'd met her, she said, "Want me to get Morley to ask his brother for you Saturday? We could double-date? Wade's the studious type and kinda shy, just like you. Even owns his own car. Bought it second-hand off a guy.''

But already I was contemplating the wards some evening soon, Laurence's shoulder casually brushing against mine.

''Oh, but it looks almost brand new. And he's really going places, that Wade. Manager of MacLeod's store, in town? Made him his assistant and Wade's only eighteen years old. So what do you say, Lorraine. Want me to?''

It would be so easy just to turn to him. ''Laurence,'' I would say, with a brilliant smile, ''I've changed my mind. I want to go sailing with you, after all.''

The Best Side of Heaven

The road we been on raggle-taggles past sagging fences, scruffy fields, and abandoned grey buildings until—just when our feet start to complain again of too much burning gravel from that bejesus hot sun—it ends, abrupt as anything, with a tree-shady lane. Then somebody's place: scabs of chalky paint shadowed over by gone-to-seed lilacs. One-and-a-half storeys, just a cottage really.

"Well, if that isn't a glorious sight," Jim says, and turns to me. Berry stains still bruise his lips from the bush where, over an hour ago, we stopped to pick lunch.

Jim's all for action. I talk too much. While I hang back trying to talk my way out of doing something dumb, Jim's off ahead quietly jumping in feet first.

We been buddies over a year now. Main friends.

"This is it!" says Jim, and swings his bundle of rags to the ground.

We travel light, Jim and me.

"You sure?" I say. "This place, Jim—maybe it's not such a good idea. See, there—somebody's tractor. Mud's not even dry on the wheels. I don't know about staying."

Not much point even to try talking. While I'm worrying about who owns the John Deere off in the field there, he pushes open the door of that little house—just like he owns it—and walks inside. I'd be a liar if I told you we haven't done this before, but the place gives me the creeps, that's for sure. I got a sixth sense about some things and I wish Jim would sometimes listen to me.

He thinks I'm a kid. I am, sort of. He's old, but he often acts like a kid because he's been in and out of the nuthouse most of his life.

"Grey Owl! It's a natural place to call home for a while. Got everything we need. Even a sink." Jim's voice rises excited, hollow-sounding, from inside, and I know I got to go and be with him.

My name's actually Johnny. My mother, back in the city, always called me that instead of John or Jack, and I got a last name too. But Jim, he's baptised me again. I'm way over half Indian. The best over-half, Jim says; and Grey Owl, he was a real famous Indian even if he was a white man.

Jim started calling me that the day he fished me out of the ditch. It was spring. I was just coming down from sniff. Jim told me I don't need sniff, the way he don't need all the pills he used to take.

"They made me crazy! What do you think of that!" He roared with laughter, a grey man, dirty as me except for two shiny gold stripes either side of his top front teeth. "I'm still crazy. Scared of me, kid?" He roared again and tossed around like some swayed-head-in-misery zoo bear. I had to laugh because I was scared not to.

"Junk," he spat on the ground. Just missed the sniff rag. "You don't need that. Know what I mean? I *am* crazy. Got that? Still. Crazy. But," he waggled his cigarette-stained fingers, "now I can think. See, that's the difference."

He sure was fired-up that day, and it made a real impression on my mind, which was still kind of cobwebby from sniff. Here he was, this total stranger, giving me hell for holding a gas-soaked rag over my nose.

I can't say I never sniffed since. At twelve years old, though, if you got nobody special and suddenly somebody wants you to act like a good person, well, all I'm saying is, you got nothing to lose by trying a little harder.

> What care I for your goose-feather bed,
> With the sheet turned down so bravely, O?
> For tonight I shall sleep in a cold, open field,
> Along with the Raggle Taggle Gypsies, O.

Jim's singing away behind the broken boarded-up windows. He thinks we're Gypsies, when he isn't telling me to be proud I'm an Indian. He goes off lots of times into these little dreams inside his head, but that's okay. We all got to have some kind of other world to take us away from this one we live in.

For me, it used to be books. That was in grade five. I read as many as ten a week until that buggering man came to live with my mother and things got so bad for a while I couldn't think much. I won't tell you all what he did to me. Jim says the best thing is to just give it a good swift kick out of my mind. "And," he says, *"no more sniff."*

The worst kind of prison there is, is the mind, Jim claims. You got to get past all that. So he teaches me old-time songs. I can even now quote from some plays, though I like best listening to Jim read the words even if I don't understand them. Sometimes he looks up and tells me what's going on. He carries around with him five by William Shakespeare. He's read to me every one. The characters have one thing in common: they're always getting stabbed or taking poison. It's a lot like real life. Back in the city, they do that all the time.

I got to say, though, our favourite is *Romeo and Juliet.* Jim dwells on the good parts. Which are the love scenes.

One day, I'd like to meet a girl like her. Man, she's some sweet chick. I figure while old Romeo lived he got to see the best side of heaven, you bet!

That's the thing about any kind of love. You don't have to have it for a lifetime for it to be good to you. And wanting it for a lifetime only gets your hopes up. I think maybe it's better to be always a little disappointed. You don't expect so much. Take what you can get and keep on moving like it's what was supposed to happen all along, that's my motto.

Inside the door the cottage is cool right away, hitting my face like it never heard winter's gone and here we are at berry time. I half expect to see a sad pile of snow over in the corner there by that dead-looking piece of long underwear. Whoever owned it is miles away from here. Years too—maybe over ten. The envelope-size calendar on the yellow door that used to close off the kitchen says, "Stiegart's Pharmacy, March 1976."

I hear Jim's boots moving loud and echoey over the floorboards above, crunching on broken glass.

Funny about abandoned houses. If they got a few things left behind, like ripped mattresses, old stoves, some little kid's broken toy, it feels emptier than if they had nothing at all. You start wondering about the people. What did they look like? What made them move away? You look for clues, like in a mystery. For instance, in one of the tight-to-open kitchen drawers, here, was left a perfectly good bottle opener. Why would she leave that? A good cook's got to have a bottle opener. Maybe where she was going she knew she could afford plenty of new ones. Maybe it reminded her of a party where things all of a sudden turned bad. Maybe she just wanted to leave something of herself because she couldn't stand to move no more.

The opener's not too rusty and it's nicer than ordinary— got a wood handle the colour of honey. I pick it up careful and put it in my pocket. It's got a new owner now.

"Jim?" I call to the floor above. Everything's still; he's stopped moving around. "What'd you find?" I go from the kitchen and start up the hallway stairs.

I blink my eyes and there's Jim at the top. Slung across his arms, held awkward like a baby he don't quite know what to do with, is a shotgun. It's old and kicked-around looking but I'm willing to bet it still works.

"Somebody's left that up there for sure. Put it back, Jim."

He smiles, holds it out. His dry white hair sticks out all over like he's charged up with electricity. "Rabbit stew," he says, nodding his head, all eager for me to want it, like it's the best present in the world.

"I don't know nothing about guns, Jim," I say, "and we shouldn't fool around with it. Put it back."

His shoulders go into a slow sag. He's like a little kid about surprises. "You're right," he says, "you're right." And turns, heavy-footed, back up the stairs.

Feeling kind of mean, I stand there, halfway up, and wait for him. He doesn't come. And he doesn't come. More than ever I want him and me out of there.

"Jim! What'd you find this time?" I'm so itchy to go my legs feel on fire.

Still no answer. I got to go all the way up the stairs in this spooky house to get him.

"Jim," I say, resting my foot on the top stair and my forehead, cool, on my hand on the dark wood banister, "let's just go, okay?"

Out of some room, moving fast, boots grinding over those glass splinters like how snow sounds when outside it's a hurting cold, he comes, this tall skinny old man. He's got arthritis in one knee, which makes him limp just a bit. "Okay, okay," he says, coming at me, pushing my chest with bony fingers. Gruff, he's back in charge. I'm happy. Because of the gun, he's decided he doesn't like this place neither.

I turn around and run back down. Jim's right behind. Even as we're going, I can feel the staircase shift and give way. I don't bother with the last six stairs, just make a jump for it and land and stagger around in time to see Jim disappear like in one of those slow-motion dreams where everything bad happens and you can't move to make it otherwise.

Heartsick, I watch the rest of the staircase cave in after him. What follows is a awful explosion. I can't believe I've heard it. He must've hid that shotgun behind his back.

"Jim, oh Jim," I say, starting to cry. "Oh Jim, oh Jim." I get belly-down and try to make some sense of all that wood collapsed into the basement. Choking dust comes up at me, and there is no light.

"Go!" he howls up from the dark. "Get somebody!"

I can't move. I pee myself.

Jim moans and howls to me again. Right away quick I take

off out of that house, down the road. I got a devil on my heels running and running. My feet go every which way. The road's blurry. A deep, squirmy pain catches my gut.

Finally a truck. It's like a holy vision coming towards me. Red. Some guy. I wave my arms. He swerves and passes. Suddenly stops. Out of the cab. He's big across and got a beer belly and he's yelling. I open my mouth and the lies start, all except for the part about Jim being hurt. He sees I been crying, that pee's made a dark circle on my pants. His voice gets soft. The questions start. Who am I? Where are my folks?

I scramble into his cab. Sit, edge of seat. We drive like crazy back towards the house.

"We got to get him to a hospital," I say, begging.

"One's just off the highway seven miles up, at Glengarry," he says, then starts again: "What the hell were you doing on my property? Who's this man you're with?" He pushes his cap back of his head. Near his eyes are bulgy veins like he's got bad nerves. "I use that gun for pickin' off *crows.* Blows them all over creation. What in Sam Hill were you doing with it?"

I look ahead and don't answer. I'm all the time thinking about social workers and welfare agencies and school and my mother and her mean-dog boyfriend. It gets all mixed up with Jim and how we got to always keep one jump ahead of everybody.

The guy pulls into the yard. We exit the cab. He heads for the house. I hang back a little. This guy'll take care of Jim. I know he won't leave him there. All along, I knew that sooner or later we'd get split up. Some winter, somewhere, he'd catch pneumonia. Or, like today, there'd be somebody asking too many questions. Find out I'm a missing kid, like the ones you see pictures of on bulletin boards. Send me back where I used to live. Social workers got it on the brain that you're always better off with your family.

I know I just got to check out. When I think this thing out clear in my head, that's the only thing to do. So I'll just walk out of the yard, hide in a ditch, and watch the truck drive past, taking Jim to Glengarry.

I can't think about him or I'll have to stay. If I think about him lying hurt in the basement. Probably be a lot of blood. I know because I saw a shotgun wound once. Blew a hole the size of a baseball in my uncle's side and he bled to death on the way to the hospital.

The hospital's where they'll take Jim. After they look after him, the nurses will give him a bath and wash and comb his wild-man's hair; and he'll lay his head back soft against a pillow. Even if he dies they'll clean him up so he looks nice.

Why do people always have to leave you out of love and a little bit of crazy? You can't find a safe place long enough for a good rest. And that's why I can't leave now. Jim's got no other safe place but me. He's got to die feeling safe. I have to be there, because what kind of friend leaves that up to strangers?

Well. They'll send me back. But at least I done this one good thing. I proved I'm a good person.

I run across the yard. The house looks at me, two beat-up windows each side of a saggy-mouth door. I think about my uncle who I didn't even like. But he was my uncle. If he'd lived he'd have been forty-three years old now. My mom's oldest brother. Everything changes. Nothing ever stays the same. Whenever things get bad Jim says we all got to adjust. I'm adjusting as best I can. But if I have to adjust much more I might just rather go join old Romeo.

Inside the house is still cold. That hasn't changed any. Just now a commotion's coming up the basement stairs. The door opens. The guy from the truck gives me a look like I'm another crow he wants to pick off, hauls his cap down over his eyes. The next thing I see, coming up behind, is Jim's head. And all of Jim! Good God, Jim! The guy, holding hard his shotgun, shoulders past me, says, "I've had a real entertaining Sunday afternoon. Now get the hell off my land." And breezes out the door.

Jim's limping more than usual and smiling like a fool. We get outside, watch the guy hoist himself, with a grunt, onto his tractor. He starts it up. How is it the sun can feel so fine?

"Thought I was dead for a minute," Jim says. He throws a raggedy arm around me, hugs me so hard that one of my ribs might snap. "Stairs collapsed, gun went off, got pinned under a wood beam. Felt like being ripped apart by hell-hounds. And what have you got there?"

"Just an old bottle opener," I tell him, flipping it into the blue blue sky and catching it, solid and real and sweet as a kiss right in the palm of my hand.

Paradise Café

Graham Sanderson said he loved me. He said it just down the road from our place, under the two-pronged cottonwood tree that looked like Paul Bunyan's arms raised in Hallelujah against the sky. He said it, between little shivering kisses that crept up the side of my neck and into my ear, so that my untouched lips felt as if they'd come into contact with a light socket.

That's how much I loved him. And I thought our love would last forever or at least six months like Barb Chappell's and Robert Maslick's had, because right after that two ducks flew up from our slough in the east field—a green head and his mate—and it was a surprisingly warm November day with magic shimmering on the golden air.

Right at the very start, after he'd noticed me (I was wearing a plaid skirt and a dark blue jersey and he was going upstairs to one class as I was coming down to another) I asked my friend Myrna what she thought of him. Myrna's forehead was high and as creamy white as a Victorian heroine's and long blue-black curls like glossy doll's hair always fell into her eyes. She tugged off a loose thread from her Perry Como sweater and said, "I've only been at the new school as long as you, Lulie, and besides, have you ever seen him without a football?"

Graham and his best friend, Neil, out in the school's field at noon hour tossing around a battered pigskin. Neil, smaller and quicker, and Graham, whose every move was sly and pondering as a hawk flying off a fencepost.

Myrna rolled over onto her back and examined her hangnails. She said, "I think Neil likes you."

The night of the Hallowe'en dance Myrna's father drove us to town in his shimmying pickup truck with the rust-lacy fenders. Myrna sank low in the cab, shielding her right eye, and I cast about for anything white to cancel the bad luck of having passed the town cemetery. Skin didn't count. Then I saw the edge of Myrna's crinoline just in time as we pulled up to the high school.

It's a good thing too, because then everything went so well that only two weeks later Graham Sanderson borrowed his grandfather's car to drive me home from school. That's when he whispered he loved me and gave me his dead father's signet ring under the cottonwood tree. I bound the back with adhesive tape and wore it on the middle finger of my left hand. Every night I whispered his name over and over to the evening star that hung like a dazzling promise above the barn rooftop.

He was my first real boyfriend, the first boy who'd ever really kissed me (unless, of course, you count Frank Pemkowski, who I let kiss me a few times in the back seat of Myrna's brother's car on account of it was good practice). I'd just turned fifteen. Girls who'd been dating since they were twelve thought I was slow or, at the very least, strange. These same girls would shriek if ever they saw anything dead or slimy or both. That's why Myrna was my friend. She wanted people to know she wasn't shocked by anything, and she'd do this by yawning and slowly stretching if, for instance, she saw two boys in a bloody fight or a cow and a bull mating. Anything like that.

Graham Sanderson's summer tan showed a white band where his father's ring had been and then his tan faded so that by mid-December you didn't notice it at all. Every Friday or Saturday night his grandfather lent him his car, and then

Graham would come from town and pick me up and we'd go back there alone or sometimes with Myrna and once we fixed her up with Neil. We went to the Rialto Theatre to see *Sabrina* with Audrey Hepburn and Humphrey Bogart, in which the chauffeur's daughter got to choose between the two sons of her father's extremely wealthy employer.

Graham thought she was too classy-looking to be a chauffeur's daughter and that the plot was far-fetched.

"Yeah, but she's Audrey Hepburn," said Myrna, outside the movie theatre. "She can go out with or marry anybody she wants."

Neil said, "I like the way the chef at her cooking school cracked an egg with one hand. Pretty neat trick. Did you notice that, Lulie?"

I told them I liked any movie starring Audrey Hepburn. Then I recounted the time, after seeing *Roman Holiday,* that I took crackers on a plate and milk in one of my mother's crystal wine glasses up to my bedroom and pretended I was a Central European princess languishing between satin sheets for the love of Gregory Peck.

Neil pushed his glasses back on his nose and said that sounded very sexy. Graham laughed and playfully punched his arm and said, "You *nimrod.*"

After that we all went over to the Paradise Café for chips and a drink. Graham said he wasn't hungry or thirsty, but he ordered for me and pulled undone the apron strings of the older girl who brought our order. She was cute in a cheap way, like a dimestore makeup queen. On her right hand was a fake gold ring. You could tell right away, because the skin around it was slightly greenish. She was wearing Topaz perfume that Neil, whispering to Myrna, said gave him a headache. I didn't like the way she kept coming back and leaning over Graham, as if he were paying for everything, and then asking if everything was "hunky-dory here."

Out on the highway, Neil and Myrna sat on opposite sides of the back seat and harmonized to "Shine on Harvest Moon" because the moon was full and they had decided to be just friends. With the car heater blasting at our knees and Graham's arm surrounding my shoulders and his head against mine, he slowly steered us home through the country night. His sweater was warm and rough against my skin and smelled of laundry soap and shaving cream. It was exactly the colour of acorns. He owned three shirts that he wore under it on alternating days. But he always wore that same sweater and it was always clean. He said it brought him good luck.

One day during the Christmas holidays, Graham showed up unexpectedly during the middle of the week. I was in the livingroom trimming the tree, a monstrous fir that grazed the ceiling.

He leaned his head against the doily on the back of my father's brown armchair and watched me on the stepladder draping the U-shaped garlands of tinsel around the tree.

"Very artistic," he said in a slow, tired voice. "You look real pretty up there." He kept his head against the doily and turned to look outside. "We haven't had a tree in a long time," he said. "Look at that snow coming down."

I steadied myself and came down the ladder. "Want to go out for a walk? It's really lovely and doesn't cost a penny."

He pushed back the sleeves of his good-luck sweater and stood up and said, "Can't. I've got to get back to town."

"How come? You just got here."

"I have to go all the same," he replied, looking down at my mouth. Suddenly he was cool and closed off. I went to hug him. He didn't want to hug me back.

"Okay, I'll see you Saturday, then," I said uncertainly. Wanting his smile, I smiled and added, "Christmas Eve, don't forget. I bought you a little something."

"Yeah. Sure," he said.

I watched him go. Past the lace curtains, the moon faintly shone in the four o'clock sky. Just a hint of shell pink delicately fringed the west over the smoky blue hump of Bison Mountain. I watched him get into his grandfather's faded ten-year-old car and pull out of our driveway. I watched until he was completely gone and all that remained were his footprints in the fresh snow and the deep circling tracks the car had made.

It had suddenly stopped snowing. Jagged frost patterns

began to ice up our livingroom windows. The wind came and covered everything over with snow. Tomorrow it would be colder.

Christmas Eve came and went and the snow came and went, harder than before until the barn roof was lumped and iced. I waited for him to come. I waited for him to call. But neither of those things happened. I had bought him a blue shirt, deep sky blue to go with his eyes and compliment the acorn shade of his good-luck sweater. Near midnight on Christmas Day the present lay under the tree, unclaimed and still wrapped.

All during that week I played my new records over and over. My new favourite song was a re-release of "Unchained Melody." I felt it had been written just for me, when the part came that went,

> And time goes by so slowly
> And time can do so much
> Are you still mine?

Now, I knew about superstitions and how silly they are. But still I said to myself, "If it snows on New Year's Eve Day, that'll mean he'll come." So I prayed to the stars out my window for snow. And the snow came! It came down heavy as popcorn stitches on a grandmother's shawl. By seven o'clock that evening I was all ready to go in a lovely black taffeta dress with a full crinkly skirt and a square neckline that made my skin look irresistible to a boy's lips. I waited by my bedroom window, waited to see his car lights come up our driveway. And they never did.

The next day, New Year's Day, I trudged three miles through the snow to Myrna's farm. She was lying on her bed, trying to feed a dried-up moth to her cat, Pinky. When she saw me, she looked grave and threw Pinky off the bed. She sat up against her pillows and when I slumped down on the end of the bed, my stocking feet on her dusky rose chenille bedspread, she pressed her toes against mine and said, "If I weren't your friend, I wouldn't tell you this, but Graham Sanderson is dating that slutty waitress from the Paradise Café. I can't believe he'd do this to you, Lulie. And with *her*, of all people."

I guess I'd have been a fool not to have guessed that

something like this had happened. Even still, my heart just died.

Back at home, in the bathroom off the kitchen, I located the German steel cuticle scissors in the soft leather case my mother had given my father for Christmas. I had never freshened the tape bound at the back of the ring. I was superstitious about taking the ring off my finger, even while washing dishes and bathing. The once-white tape was frayed and grey and caked as a miniature Egyptian mummy. I hacked away with the scissors until the decayed cloth came away. I attacked with rubbing alcohol the white crud still clinging to the silver. In the kitchen I located a can of liquid Silvo and a soft cloth and rubbed the ring until the initials P.S.—from a dead man I'd never known—came gleaming back when held to the sun. In a clean white piece of tissue paper I wrapped the ring, still warm from my hand, over and over, then dropped it into a box and put that box into a larger box. I wrapped it all up in brown paper, wrote Graham Sanderson's address on the front with no return address, mailed it, and vowed never to speak to him again.

The following Saturday, Neil came by in his father's new Buick. We drove to town for a short while. He asked if I would like to go to the Valentine Dance at the school with him in one month's time. I said sure, might as well. So Neil took me to the dance and brought me home again.

When I casually mentioned that we hadn't seen Graham there, he bluntly said, "He didn't appreciate you, Lulie. I know how things are tough for him and his mom, and that his grandfather wouldn't let him use the car anymore. But I'd have gotten a job. Anything—just to be able to afford the gas to keep coming out here to see you." Then he kissed me and held me and kissed me again and asked me to be his girl. All the time he was doing this, I kept my eyes open wide. He said I was the classiest girl he'd ever met and over his shoulder, out the car window, the moon shone mercilessly down on the cottonwood tree, on its shivering, naked, up-reaching arms.

The Crystal Stars
Have Just Begun To Shine

L isa Barnett, moving down the halls, books clasped
against her chest, tosses tawny hair away from her
eyes in one fluid motion.

How does she do that? Just once I'd like to be able to do
that. I have this wild frizzy hair that my boyfriend, Brad,
says drives him crazy with unrequited passion, and then he
leans me back in his arms and his bicycle topples to the
ground. Brad's hair is black with a dyed green stripe down
the centre. Brad is half Japanese.

My dad is Jamaican. His hair is more agreeable than
mine—always soft, like he's just been caught in the rain.
My Mom's hair, I can see in photos, is much like Lisa Barnett's, although it could be any colour now. Who knows?
I don't remember her except for the photos. She was young
and pretty when she checked out.

A thought strikes! Lisa Barnett could look like my half-
sister. The one I've never met.

The stereotypical image of the Jamaican male is that he
is a perennial adolescent who is never at home, a poor
provider, a skirt-chaser who leaves all the child-rearing up

to his bossy wife. My Auntie Eulie, Daddy's sister, is actually married to a man like that. I wouldn't give you two cents for Uncle Gilbert. Neither, I think, would Auntie Eulie. Except she's stuck with him.

Daddy is sometimes a terrible yeller and sometimes a hugger. In between times, he's quite reserved. At night, he sits alone in his armchair and watches reruns of *M*A*S*H*. He gets up every morning and goes to a job he hates. He buys the best of everything he can afford for us and has an aversion to leftovers. So I always eat them cold for breakfast before I go to school; this helps ease my sense of guilt.

I feel guilty a lot. I sometimes even feel guilty that I was born. Then I feel guilty about feeling guilty about that because after he's yelled, when I'm bent over homework and stuffing my face with a snack, he comes up behind me, wraps his arms around my shoulders, and mumbles parental anguish. I'm gumming a mouthful of chips and there he is, rocking me cheek to cheek, telling me I'm all he's got.

It's hell being loved by someone who spends his whole miserable life just looking after you. I wish he had a girlfriend. But he rarely goes out, that's how much of a rut he's in. A couple of years ago I came home from a movie and he and this woman were sitting in the living room, drinking beer, all cuddled up on the couch with the TV blaring. She was a redhead. She smiled at me and I immediately liked her. I was so relieved to see him with somebody. But he was embarrassed. As if a parent, for pete's sake, isn't supposed to have feelings like the rest of us mortals. After that night I didn't see the redhead again. I was so disgusted with him I never asked who she was or where she'd come from.

Brad, my boyfriend, says it's probably just that he's too old now to enjoy women.

"My God," I tell him, "he's only forty-six!"

"So," he shrugs, "let's fix him up with somebody."

"Like who?"

"I dunno. We must know somebody who's as old as him."

Daddy's sparkling social life suggests a handful of possibilities. We start eliminating the implausibles and what remains is Rita, the over-permed check-out lady at Payfair. She looks to be about his age and is friendly, kind, divorced, and available. I have, however, one reservation. She's rather flabby. I feel that if we're going to set my father up with a woman, she's got to be in good shape.

"Why?" says Brad. "I don't see your dad out jogging and he drives a bus all day long."

"He's perfectly fit," I say protectively.

"He's got a paunch," Brad says cruelly, and smiles. He has these marvellous eyebrows, like wings; they move about at will. When he's excited, his whole face looks as if at any moment it'll take off somewhere.

"You have to face facts, Deirdre," he says, leaning over the counter in his mother's kitchen, where we're sitting on high stools as we pig out on Calamato olives and oatmeal biscuits that Brad himself has made. He plants me with a nice cozy kiss. "Look," he continues, "Rita doesn't exactly make *me* sweat. But who knows what she'll do for your father?"

"Maybe he'd be better off with Auntie Eulie's friend Ginny after all," I muse. "She's better looking. Besides, she's black. A change, they say, is as good as a rest."

"Ginny, as we have already discussed, is wacko," says Brad. "She's desperate and totally unstable. Would you want her for a stepmother?"

In spite of Brad's green hair, he's really a very straight-ahead guy. He thinks all love relationships should end happily in marriage. His Italian mother and Japanese father have been married over twenty-three years. He says from the minute he laid eyes on me he knew we were right for each other. He had his mother work out our astrological signs, and according to the reading ours would be a marriage made in heaven. I told him to quit talking that way, we're only fourteen. He responded, wiggling his eyebrows, "In seven years I'm going to marry you, Deirdre, so don't argue with Destiny."

My father does most of our grocery shopping at Payfair. Sometimes I go with him. He shops every Thursday evening after supper. He makes a list, carefully marking off with a little red tick each of the specials he's seen advertised at other stores. Then he can comparison shop. At the store he checks prices according to units instead of by weight. When he shops he looks like the male version of a bag lady. He is one very drab dude. You have to imagine a skinny balding black man (with a *slight* paunch) in a shapeless camel coat (Zellers special, 1979), wine-coloured polyester slacks, and black rubber galoshes.

"You're going to have to do something about the clothes, Deirdre," says Brad. "Doesn't he own anything that looks modern?"

"I gave him jeans for Christmas last year. He never wears them," I say, suddenly discouraged.

"Make him wear the jeans Thursday night. And does he own a decent sweater—or anything?"

"Only a navy turtleneck Auntie Eulie gave him to go with the jeans," I say. "He's never worn that either."

Thursday night I make dinner and invite Brad to stay. Daddy gets home and kisses my forehead and asks Brad if he's ever considered dying his green stripe orange. He laughs all the way to the bathroom, where he washes up. Then he goes to his bedroom to change. I go and tap lightly on his door. "Daddy," I say, "please don't wear those purple pants tonight."

"What's wrong with the purple pants?" he says from behind the door.

"They're so tacky."

"They're perfectly fine, I wear them all the time," he says, indignant and ready to yell.

"Exactly," I snap back. "And I get tired of looking at you in them. It's time you changed your image. Get reckless." Sometimes, if I state my mind firmly enough, he comes through.

Dead silence from behind the door. Then a suspicious, "Why are you all of the sudden so concerned about the way I look?"

"The jeans," I say. "Okay?"

"They're obscenely tight, Deirdre," he says coldly.

"They're supposed to be tight. That's how they're worn. Are you going to wear those purple pants until you drop dead? I'll have to bury you in them."

"All right," he mutters, "all right."

I stay by the door, breathing.

"What else?" he says.

"Else?"

"What else do you want me to wear. With the tight jeans."

"Oh," I say, as casually as possible, "well, what about that nice sweater Auntie Eulie gave you?"

Another silence.

"It itches," he whines.

"Wear an undershirt," I say, and quickly leave.

He appears, five minutes later, looking uncomfortable and handsome.

Brad stares at him, obviously amazed. Daddy gives him the cold eye and flares up. "What're you gawking at? It's my fashion statement."

"Terrific," says Brad. Later, in the car, he whispers out of the corner of his mouth, "For God's sake make sure he takes off that coat when we get there."

Rita smiles warmly as we trail snow through the door. She doesn't appear to be busy tonight. She's running through a litre of milk for an old lady with an English accent.

"Hi Rita!" Brad and I say, almost in unison. Daddy scurries off to get his cart. He hasn't even acknowledged her.

"Love in bloom," says Brad sarcastically, as we traipse after Daddy.

"I'll attend to his coat," I say, ignoring this. "Your job is the candies."

In the produce section Daddy pauses over bags of celery. He lifts several, checking each for weight. Light celery is stringy, heavy celery is succulent. He frowns, decides against buying celery this week, and moves on to the broccoli, where he scrutinizes the heads through his half-glasses. Brad has disappeared. I imagine him whisking back down Aisle 2 so he'll come out directly in front of Rita's till. Now, he's reaching into his jacket. He produces the heart-shaped box of chocolates we bought earlier in the day at the drugstore. It didn't look too fresh, but what can you do? This is November and they're probably a holdover from last Valentine's day. But the heart shape was absolutely essential, you see, because older ladies really like that kind of stuff.

"They sure keep this store hot, don't they?" I say to Daddy.

"Huh?" He's carefully shaking out a plastic produce bag.

"Want me to hold your coat?"

"Why would I want you to hold my coat?" He eases two stalks of broccoli into the bag.

I see I'm going to have to be more forceful. "Daddy, for heaven's sake, you look like a bag lady in that coat. What will people think? Do you want to embarrass me?"

He takes off his glasses, waves them impatiently around. "Deirdre, what on earth are you talking about? What people? Do you see any people in this store? There are no people. None."

"Well...there could be. There might be. *Anybody* could walk through that door, right now."

"Tsk!"says Daddy, scowling. But he unbuttons the coat before moving on to the apples. His sweater and jeans are at least visible.

Brad slips up behind me just as we progress to the canned goods.

"That took long enough," I whisper tensely.

We hang back like a couple of thieves. Daddy is checking out the canned tomatoes.

"She's terrific!" says Brad, eyebrows poised for lift-off. "I mean, up until now I must admit I've totally overlooked her personality and her eyes. She's got great eyes! But if I was an older man—yeah! I'd take a chance on her myself."

"I want to know her reaction, Brad."

"Shock."

"Good or bad?" I say, watching his face carefully.

"At first it was hard to tell. She just froze with this blank expression. I then told her he was too shy to give them to her himself but that she could thank him personally when she rang up his groceries."

"What'd she say?"

"Nothing. Believe it or not, she smiled like she'd just been handed a ticket to Florida. Your father has something I've missed." He waves at Daddy who, cautious, still scowling, holds aloft a large can of stewed tomatoes.

"I don't see why you're so surprised," I say haughtily. One down. One to go. Please God, let him be smiling when he gets to Rita's till. If you do, I'll eat cold pork every morning for the next month.

Fifteen minutes before closing, Daddy has finally put the last item in his cart. He wheels it over to Rita's till. She nods and smiles enigmatically.

"Evening Rita," he says, throwing down a two-pound tub of Monarch margarine.

She rings it through. I notice she's freshly applied dark pink lipstick. My father makes a remark about the weather and stares dismally past her shoulder out the window at the snow that is singing against the glass.

Wordlessly, Rita rings through the rest of the groceries. I've never noticed how much better she looks up close than far away. Up close you really *can* see that her best feature is her eyes. They're pale amber with thick lashes. Her nose is perhaps too big, her skin sort of saggy. But those eyes! She really talks with them. Too bad all this seems to be lost on Daddy. If he'd only look directly at her he'd see what's there.

Just when I think we're never going to get this show on the road, she rings up the bill and, as Daddy hands her three twenty-dollar bills, sort of leans into him and whispers, practically in his ear, "Thanks for the box of chocolates, Elliot. It really made my day."

Daddy doesn't move. He seems paralyzed, except for his eyes, which shift upward to her, back to us, then dart wildly about the store as he processes this information. Finally he takes off his glasses, seems about to say something, and can't. He looks back at her, smiles. She smiles back. Her eyes do a bit of talking. Daddy's eyes start doing their own talking.

I never knew this would be so embarrassing! I can't watch them anymore so I turn around to Brad who still is. Mesmerized, he wears a foolish smile.

I wish somebody would say something out loud. Nobody does. Eventually we leave, each holding onto bags of groceries. Our warm breath hits the outside air and searches out the night. Overhead the crystal stars have just begun to shine.

About the Author

Martha Brooks was born and raised in a tuberculosis sanitorium near Ninette, Manitoba, where her father was the chief surgeon. She began writing after the birth of her daughter sixteen years ago. Her first novel, *A Hill for Looking* (Queenston House, 1982), was based on one year of her childhood, and was short-listed for the Canadian Library Association's Children's Book of the Year Award. She lives in Winnipeg and has taught creative writing in Manitoba schools for seven years. She is also an accomplished playwright, whose works have been commissioned by the Prairie Theatre Exchange in Winnipeg and toured across the country.